AMONG THE FOUNDERS

D. E. ANDERSON

Among the Founders

Produced and printed by Stillwater River Publications.

Visit our website at
www.StillwaterPress.com
for more information.

First Stillwater River Publications Edition

ISBN: 978-1-958217-58-0

1 2 3 4 5 6 7 8 9 10
Written by D. E. Anderson
Cover & interior book design by Matthew St. Jean
Published by Stillwater River Publications,
Pawtucket, RI, USA

I wish to dedicate this book to everyone that believed in me and helped push me to finish my first ever novel.

I want to give a special thanks to my wife because without her, I would have never actually finished this book. I also want to give a special thanks to the rest of my family as you all urged me to follow my dreams and that is something that I will never be able to thank you all enough for.

I love you all.

Thank you for everything you've done for me.

1

The deer bowed its head as it tore stray blades of grass into its mouth. Its tail flicked away at the stray flies buzzing around while its eyes searched for its next snack, though it would not even have enough time left in its life to finish the one it had just pulled from the earth.

Despite being a typical deer, it was more valuable than gold, and was most likely the last deer in the area for at least twenty miles.

As a result of lethal levels of pollution causing the collapse of ecosystems around the globe, the deer, along with most of the other animals on the planet, nearly went extinct stemming from the Earth's biggest parasite: the human race.

It all began with an unforeseen major population boom. As a result, people had a dramatic increase in their consumption of energy and other resources that the planet had to offer, draining everything of use. It only grew worse as they realized how much waste they were creating. Ecosystems were now only toxic waste yards and the rest of the soil on the planet was so over-saturated with toxicity, that fruits and vegetables couldn't be eaten unless they were grown from clean soil. If grown in plain soil, the food contained the toxins that would inevitably kill the consumer.

However, with the human race being brought to near extinction and not causing further damage, in only a few decades the planet was already making large strides in healing itself.

In an ironic twist, animals had evolved to be able to safely process the toxins from their food and water. Subtle changes to their lungs and liver allowed their numbers to increase again. Humans on the other hand were losing numbers as they faced starvation, plagues, decreased life expectancy from carcinogens in the air and wars as the world leaders began to point fingers at one another in blame for the damage to the planet.

When humanity first realized they were staring at mass extinction, they formed small pods called Communities stocked with their remaining supplies, technology, and the few lucky families that were chosen to repopulate the planet. As years went on, these Communities too collapsed from starvation, war, and sickness. After 120 years of struggling, now in the year 2929, there remains only one barely surviving Community, Community: 1049.

And one of its people had the deer in his sights.

The nineteen-year-old man named Lance released the breath he was holding in his chest just as the nocked arrow effortlessly took flight from his fingertips, cutting through the air, and piercing the heart of the deer upon impact. It dropped dead instantly before it could register what had just happened with the half-chewed lump of grass hanging lazily from its mouth. Lance let the soles of his boots slide off the rough bark of the branch from which he was perched. He hit the ground on one knee and gracefully rose to a standing position. He shouldered his wooden bow and approached his kill. He frowned and pulled the stone-tipped arrow from the animal's limp body. He hated killing animals, but he, his family, and his people needed to eat. It was an unfortunate and necessary evil.

This was the first deer he had seen in almost three weeks. There had been some small game unlucky enough to cross his path, but nothing substantial enough as to what would constitute a "full meal" for everyone back home. This would feed and clothe some at least, but it wouldn't be enough to feed the three hundred or so people of the Community. Lately, the scraps of food they had been surviving on was barely enough to quiet their growling stomachs. Winter was on the way and the majority of the animals in the area had been practically hunted out, and those that hadn't been were moving on to warmer places. Those needing warmer clothing would be fighting over the scraps of fur-lined leather clothing that the leather worker would prepare once the animals were gutted, or as Lance preferred, "cleaned".

Lance believed more and more each passing day that there were more animals beyond what his people called, "the Edge"—which was the edge of the forest cluster in which they hunted within. Even though he had the opportunity to go look for himself every day without anyone knowing, he never did as he knew he had been forbidden to do so by the leaders of Community: 1049—the Elders. From the time he was a child capable of understanding the words of those around him, it was drilled into his mind that there was nothing except death waiting for anyone that dared to trespass beyond the forest's edge as pollution was supposed to be worse past their borders.

As of late, Lance wasn't sure if he could believe the Elders, but he had no evidence that it wasn't safe to go beyond the Edge. But if you asked him he would admit that what was truly holding him back from looking was the possibility that the Elders could be right and he would only be walking into his death, and to him, that was a gamble not worth taking, just yet anyways.

A strong hand patted Lance warmly on the shoulder jarring him from his thoughts. "Nice shot," his mother, Shushannah congratulated. He shook her hand off with a grunt. "What the hell? I was just giving you a goddamned compliment," she snarled.

Lance was built to be the perfect hunter. He was quick and nimble with broad shoulders and was silent and methodical when tracking prey. In fact, he took pride in being one of the few people to sneak up on his mother. The only thing holding him back from excelling as a hunter was that he hated killing the animals. In the past, when food wasn't hard to come by, and would instead occupy himself in a tree with a book, lost to the world around him. His mother had caught him once or twice, scaring him out of the tree and yelling at him until her face was blue.

Lance was well aware of his mother's disappointment in him as she had always been vocal with her opinions, but she was still proud to call him her son. He was still out there with her day in and day out and doing what needed to be done when it was needed. Despite that though, there was always a sliver of distrust towards him when they came back from their hunts, especially now with animals being so scarce and so many hungry mouths waiting for them at home. She needed to be sure that he was all in just like she was. When they went into the woods, they weren't a mother and son anymore, they were hunters and needed to act that way. Their conversations on the way home were more like interrogations as she tore into her son making sure he left no stone unturned. Only when he brought more animals back than her did they speak of niceties.

Lance noted to himself that his mother was sporting a belt packed full of small game swaying lifelessly back and forth. Some flies were beginning to gather around a few of the squirrels, landing on their fur and rubbing their grubby little hands together.

His mother's sandy hair, the same shade as Lance's, was pulled back into a tight bun to keep the strands out of her face. Oftentimes his father, Marick, would pull Lance's own long hair back and joke about the two being twins as they shared the same pointed facial features, and sometimes, the same scowl.

"Yeah," Lance grumbled, "But you know I hate killing animals, yet you still make a spectacle of it, like I should *celebrate* what I just did."

"Fine. If you don't like being a hunter, maybe you should change careers then. Why don't you go apprentice with the leather worker and makes shoes all day?" she huffed, "What you just did *is* worth celebrating! That's less people going to bed with empty stomachs tonight!"

Lance gave her a sideways glare as rage boiled underneath his flesh. He hoisted the deer over his shoulder with an audible grunt. It wasn't the biggest he'd ever taken down, weighing just under a hundred pounds he guessed, but it certainly wasn't small. He had half the amount of animals around his belt than what his mother had on hers. He noticed her gaze fall and rise again to his face but she didn't say anything.

"Let's get back to the Community," Lance mumbled before quickly stepping past his mother and ignoring her previous comment, "Your squirrels are attracting friends."

They silently walked back home, with Lance leading the way, setting the pace since he had the heaviest load to carry. He could feel his mother's stare boring into his back the whole trip home.

They could hear a dull roar from Community: 1049 well before they were able to see it, which made Lance wonder if it was the noise driving away any potential animals in the area or if they just *were* being hunted out.

He remembered the first hunting lesson that his mother had given him when he was just about ten years old. He had stepped on a branch just before his mother was able to take a shot at a deer, scaring it away. She spun on her heel with fury burning in her eyes. "You will do well to watch where you walk out here. That was dinner tonight and you just scared it off. It's probably at least a mile away from here now." That was one of the most important lessons he learned as a hunter: noise never fits into the equation when hunting.

He knew he was grasping at straws. Humans were paying for what they did to the planet and it didn't matter what the cause was, the fact of the matter was that there was no food anymore. They wouldn't last like this much longer. It was penance for the behavior of their ancestors.

They walked through the gate and passed by the guards armed with heavy clubs and their bulky plastic armor. Lance would love to be a guard at the gate. There wasn't a damned thing to guard except the dirt and trees, but in the event of a bear or wolf stumbling upon their home, it was nice knowing someone was there to watch out. But there was no way Lance could ever be a guard.

The gates themselves to enter the Community consisted of a heavily rusted iron fence that wrapped around the grounds of the entire compound where they met at an open mouth that was always guarded since a wolf snuck in a few years ago and ran off with a young child. There was only the one entrance located at the front of the compound, but it was still pretty easy to sneak in and out over the fence as long as there was something to stand on. Sometimes it was just nice to listen to the sounds of the forest and get away from everyone else to think for a while.

Upon seeing the deer, one of the guard's eyes widened, while the other looked as if he could eat the beast raw. Lance gave them a courteous nod in greeting. The guards could make life a living hell if you were on their bad side, but if you were on their good side they often let you get by with little more than a slap on the wrist. It was easier for Lance and Shushannah to find themselves on their bad side though since they were what the Community considered "Outsiders", so Lance tried to be as nice as possible to them—not that it helped him much growing up with all the trouble he found himself in.

The name "Outsider" originated well before Lance's lifetime as a way to describe those living outside of the massive structure that they call the Alabaster Rampart which is where the Community was first established. There was a village of about a hundred people or so on the outside of the giant building, constructed of lumber they made cutting down trees when the Alabaster Rampart couldn't comfortably keep everyone inside. Those that were able to stay inside refer to themselves as "Insiders", or their preferred title "Founders", as they were the direct descendants of the original families that made up the Community. They were generally not the type to be trusted if you were an Outsider as they viewed Outsiders as nothing more than a waste of space and an eyesore.

In the Old World, the Alabaster Rampart was a hospital that

treated the mentally ill, but it now was the home for the Founders. The emblem design on the tile floor of the front lobby inside still read, "Canterbury Asylum" with the words circling around what looked like a blueberry bush, but everyone still referred to it as the Alabaster Rampart. It was a giant wall of white with vines climbing up its sides all the way to the roof. Lance used to be afraid of the large building when he was young, but he soon learned that it was not the building to be feared, but the people *inside* of it.

Despite this stance, Lance's best friend, Wallais, was a Founder, but he certainly didn't act like one as he treated everyone he met with the same respect they treated him with. He and his family didn't believe in labels. Unfortunately, people like Wallais's family were far and few. Regardless of the important roles that Lance's family held in the Community, they were still looked at sideways.

Lance and his mother passed through the center of the little makeshift village and made their way to the Rampart. The deer and small game were to be delivered directly to the cook in the kitchens, Gordin. The little, greasy man would be pleased to finally see some meat to cook. The sad, grayish vegetables that were being brought to him by the Community's plant growers were little more than tasteless, nutrition-less, pieces of rubber and served only as a weak attempt to quiet the rumbling stomachs of the people for a short while. Due to the lack of food, he was forced to let most of his staff go since there wasn't anything to cook other than the massive cauldron of perpetual stew and that didn't need a team of ten to manage as at this point it was mostly just a depressing, flavorless gray broth with scraps of carrot and peppers floating sporadically around that he stirred on occasion to make sure nothing inside burned.

As the pair passed through the front lobby to the back of the building they could feel the disdainful glares from the Founders lingering on them as they went through despite the deer over Lance's shoulder. Their leather, hand-made clothing stood out among the more professionally woven clothes the Founders treated themselves to that visibly acted as their badge of honor. Despite still having an abundance of wool for the looms to last them at least another century, they refused to make any clothing for the Outsiders.

The kitchens were kept just as clean as the rest of the building—immaculate. Gordin, usually stood out from the kitchen as his clothing was always covered in stains of some kind. He typically scurried around—similar to a spooked squirrel—when there was a lot of cooking to be done. But when he wasn't cooking, he was mostly doing what Lance and Shushannah found him doing when they walked into the kitchen. He had his face resting lazily in one hand while the other spun aimlessly around on a shining aluminum counter with a dry rag. He was staring off into space and gave no indication that he noticed the pair had come in. Lance found it depressing to see the man like this. Normally he was so full of life, but the way things have been lately was putting a damper on everyone's mood—even the happiest of the bunch.

Then an idea crossed his mind.

With an evil grin, Lance slammed the dead deer down as hard as he could on the counter behind Gordin, causing him to yelp and flail awkwardly away from the table. A wild look flashed into his eyes and then quickly faded when he saw who it was. He smiled. "You son of a bitch," he chuckled, pointing at Lance. They embraced in greeting. "You scared the hell out of me. C'mere, Shannah." He gave Shushannah a tight hug too which she reciprocated with a small frown of disgust upon realizing she put her hand in a damp spot of sweat on his back. She had put her own haul on the table as well once she stepped back.

"We had a good hunt this morning," she beamed with pride, "Best one in weeks I'd say. I can't wait to try some stew tonight."

"Yeah, I'm starving. I'm tired of having just carrot bits with warm water," Lance mumbled.

Gordin grinned as he spoke. "Well, with all this meat it will definitely taste like soup again, even if only for a short while. Good job guys! I was starting to lose my mind down here with nothing to do."

Lance shrugged. "Hey, I just need to get some food in me to be honest. At this point I'm ready to start chewing on tree bark."

The trio laughed, but it was half-hearted as the unspoken reality of the situation had already set in for them. Starvation was inching closer and closer every day. Unfortunately, nobody knew what they could do to fix things. The Community was waiting on word from the Elders for an answer to their problems, but so far, there was nothing but silence from them, which was most unusual. People were beginning to talk amongst themselves, doubting their leadership. If the problem didn't get addressed soon, there was going to be a fissure in the Community, just like all the others before theirs, causing a collapse and destroying their home, leaving it nothing more than a forgotten memory.

"Have Ogden and Seamus come by yet?" Lance asked, curious about what they were able to find.

Ogden, Wallais's father, and Seamus, Wallais's brother, were also hunters in the group with Lance and Shushannah and the only pair out of their modest group of eight that they were friendly with. Ogden was a fun person to be around—if you weren't Lance. Ogden had a habit of what he believed was lightheartedly slapping Lance on the shoulder when he would first greet him. As Ogden was a large fellow, Lance would feel the massive clap on his shoulder for hours and genuinely feared what Ogden's true strength felt like. Having a different, and much less agile stature, paired with the boisterous noise wherever he went, it was a blunder to Lance how he was able to bring back anything when he would go out. His son, Seamus, was the exact opposite. He was quiet, small, and certainly didn't slap Lance when he saw him. He was a pretty relaxed guy and usually kept to himself.

"Nope. I haven't seen them yet today. I'm sure they can't be far behind. It's about mid-afternoon now, right? I can't see anything in this damned basement."

"Yes, it is," Shushannah answered, "We have to pick up Adelade soon. I don't want to be late again. Poor Beatrice has her hands full with those runts."

Lance agreed with her. They weren't always on time to pick up his little sister from school. Adelade didn't mind waiting though because she enjoyed Beatrice's company, but Beatrice often wanted to get home and relax after watching the other thirty or so kids in the class. Being such a sweet woman, she never complained about watching Adelade a little longer than the other kids, but both Shushannah and Lance knew deep inside she just wanted to be rid of all the kids as soon as she could. As she is Wallais's mother, they felt more comfortable leaving Adelade with her, which often meant they would lose track of time since she never complained.

Lance's little eight-year-old sister Adelade was as close to perfect as one could find among the people of Community: 1049, though Lance was sure it stemmed from the fact that she was sheltered. His parents thought it was best that she try to remain a child for as long as possible, but Lance was beginning to wonder lately how good this was for her in the long run. If things took a turn for the worst, how were they going to be able to tell her? She had been viewing the world through a foggy lens and he believed that it would only hurt her later on. He wanted to tell her about all the nights he and his parents skipped their dinner so that she wouldn't be hungry or about what people inside of the Alabaster Rampart were really like. This was not the world to raise a sheltered child in and she needed to know the harsh realities just like he did.

Lance's stomach gave an aggravated moan. His train of thought reminded him that last night was his turn to go without supper. He wouldn't be skipping anything tonight though. He was even debating on working up the gall to ask for a second bowl if he could eat the first one fast enough.

"Yeah, we should get going. See you later, Gordin," he said, turning to leave the kitchens.

"Bye guys! Thanks again for the meat," Gordin called behind them.

They left the kitchens and lugged their exhausted bodies back up the stairs to the top floor while they could hear Gordin chuckle joyfully behind them with clattering knives hitting the table while he prepared to clean the deer and dice up the meat. Lance's mouth began to water as he thought of digging into the stew later.

The Community's school was actually a room used for the education of patients back when the facility was still running, so it was fairly well-equipped to teach kids of all ages. Everyone in the Community attends school in the same room no matter where you live or what "social opinions" your family may have. Sometimes those "opinions" would leak into class when a child would let a comment or two slip, but Beatrice was quick to put a stop to it, despite knowing it was a losing battle. The kids learned it all from their parents who would be teaching hate to their children. Beatrice just wanted a safe place for *all* the children of the Community to learn.

Their boots clicked along the tile floor as they walked in tandem. They kept their heads low and stayed at a brisk pace while avoiding the looks from Founders standing inside of the doorways to their apartment rooms or while they walked the halls, stopping to look and wonder why they were inside. Lance wasn't fully paying attention to where he was going and roughly bumped into someone. He bounced backwards and gave a quick, "Sorry," without looking up and tried to continue along his way.

"Watch where you're going asshole," the man growled. Lance instantly recognized the voice and turned on his heel, his blood firing up again. The voice belonged to a Founder named Jasper who was one of the people Lance hated the most. Shushannah tried to pull Lance along, but he brushed her off, his anger clouding his judgment.

"Who are you calling an asshole?" Lance fired back-stepping closer to Jasper.

Jasper stood eye-to-eye with Lance. They had the same athletic build, but Jasper had short dark hair, a clean-shaven face and piercing blue eyes. He was the son of one of the Elders—Elder Maxwell, but that didn't stop Lance from backing down from a fight with him. Everyone else did *except* him and Jasper really hated it. Ever since they were kids, Jasper and Lance were at each other's throats and could hardly stand to be in the same room as one another. Beatrice actually had to confine them to opposite sides of the classroom, but even then that was hardly able to keep them from bickering or worse, like when a chair was thrown.

It started back in their school days when Lance embarrassed Jasper by correcting him in class, which caused giggles among their peers. Jasper couldn't stand being shown up by an Outsider, so he took his revenge by bribing two other kids in their class to help him beat up Lance. Ever since that day they hated each other.

"Fuck off, Jasper. Lance, let's go, we need to get your sister," Shushannah hissed.

"Aw, how cute. You have your mommy fight your battles," Jasper teased with a smirk.

"I've kicked your ass before. I'll do it again," Lance threatened, moving his face barely an inch away from Jasper's.

Jasper's face flustered and he set his jaw. Lance knew he was remembering a few years back when Jasper fought him one-on-one instead of three-on-one with whoever else felt like beating up an Outsider, and Lance had knocked him out by bouncing his head off of the corner of a door. A couple of other Founders dragged him off before anyone else could see him. Lance was stuck with clean up duty in the kitchens for that, but he would have done dishes a thousand times over just to see Jasper passed out on the ground again like that.

Jasper swung wildly at Lance, but Lance managed to dodge it before it was able to connect with the right side of his face. He recoiled back and was about to retaliate when Shushannah grabbed his arm.

"No," she growled, "Let's go! Stop acting like a couple of children!"

Lance gritted his teeth and refused to break his stare from Jasper. Jasper was breathing heavily, his fingers working feverishly at his sides from the adrenaline. A crowd had gathered around them looking to see what the commotion was about. Shushannah pulled on Lance's hand to keep him going. She was right. A fight would only cause more problems for them.

He turned his back to Jasper without uttering another syllable.

Every atom in his body wanted to turn around and cave in Jasper's face with his fist, but he kept himself under control by biting his tongue and taking some breaths through his nose.

"Yeah, walk away! We'll finish this later, Momma's Boy," Jasper called with a chuckle, putting on a show for the people. Lance could picture the smug grin on Jasper's face which only infuriated him more.

"Fuck him. Don't listen to him. He isn't worth the trouble."

"I'd take whatever punishment the Elders gave me. I don't care. He makes my blood boil."

"I agree, but his father is one of the leaders of our Community. We're already in their line of fire for being Outsiders and I don't want to give them more ammunition against us. Not to mention the fact that you're an adult and somewhat of a role model for the younglings. *Adelade included.*"

"But he's such a dickhead," Lance growled.

"Again, I agree, but there isn't anything we can do. We have to just keep our heads down and do our part."

Lance scoffed. It was all bullshit. He hated being dirt.

"Come on. School is probably out by now. I don't want Beatrice to have to wait around for us."

They hurried on ahead, now at a jog instead of a brisk pace, to the designated school room.

Before they could make it down the hallway, a little pony-tailed blonde girl came running up shouting, "Lance!" She leapt into his arms and wrapped around his torso tightly. Little Adelade was his world and her hugs always made him feel better. He returned her hug with one equally as tight before setting her down and already beginning to forget about his run in with Jasper.

"Hello! How was your day?" He planted a kiss on the top of her head. Shushannah did the same with a smile. Beatrice came over and hugged them with her usual happy demeanor.

"It was so great! We learned about dinosaurs! Did you know that they were like big lizards?"

The little girl's eyes were the size of saucers. Whenever she got excited about something her eyes grew at least three times their normal size. Last week it was when they learned about ants and now it was dinosaurs. Lance remembered being just like her when he was that age, thinking that it was magical to learn about the world. He knew it would only be a matter of time before that knowledge began to disappoint her just as it did himself.

"Hello Shushannah, Lance. How was the hunt today?"

Lance gave a shrug and a forced smile.

"It was great," Shushannah answered ignoring Lance's face, "Lance took down a deer with some other smaller game and I got about five or six rodents. The stew will finally have some meat tonight for the first time in weeks!"

Beatrice smiled at Shushannah while her eyes quickly darted over to Lance. She was aware, like everyone he was close with, that he didn't take joy in hunting like his mother did. She had offered him a job as a teacher numerous times in the past, but he refused as he couldn't stand little kids other than Adelade. He couldn't understand why their hands were *always* sticky no matter how many times they were cleaned. Plus, their parents wouldn't be too thrilled about an "Outsider" teaching their kids. It was bad enough for them that the kids were "mixed in" he heard a parent say one day.

Her eyes said, "The teaching offer still stands if you change your mind."

He'd rather eat worms before teaching those little bastards. He remembered what it was like in that room growing up. Those kids were animals. He would pull all his hair out before the end of his first week. No way, he enjoyed the peacefulness of his walks too much to throw that away.

"That's good. It'll be nice to have something other than rubbery vegetable scraps in water. Have you seen Wallais yet today?" Beatrice questioned, changing the subject much to Lance's approval.

"Nope. I was thinking of stopping over to the gardens for a visit," Lance answered, relieved to be moving on.

"I think he would like that. Things have been rough down there. Well, I'm sure you know. Your father is down there with him."

"I'll have to do that then. My visits always cheer him up," he remarked sarcastically.

Beatrice gave him a warm smile. She was the sweetest woman in the entire Community for sure. She was like a second mom to him all the years that he had been friends with Wallais and the rest of their family.

"Mommy, I'm tired. Can we go home now?" Adelade whined.

"Alright," Shushannah breathed. She was holding the little girl's hand gently in hers.

Adelade smiled up at her. She was the only person in the world that had an ounce of power over Shushannah. He didn't know what it was, but she always had their mother wrapped around her little finger. Lance had to admit he was a little jealous of his sister for having that effect on his mother. He was never treated that way when he was her age. His father was far kinder to him than his mother growing up.

"I'll take this one home. I'll see you soon, Lance. Tell Wallais I say 'Hi.'" Shushannah and Adelade waved goodbye and proceeded back down the hall towards home.

"Can I speak to you?" Beatrice asked in a whisper.

"Of course! What's on your mind?"

"I didn't want to talk about this in front of Adelade. I don't know how much you all like her to know or not know. There's been... *talk* that the Elders are going to have a solution to our hunger problem, and it doesn't bring good tidings for you or your family.

2

"What do you mean?" Lance shifted on his feet nervously, bracing himself for the worst.

Beatrice usually had a kind, welcoming face, but immediately after Lance asked his question, her face fell a grave expression took its place. Her lips pursed, and her eyes grew anxious, darting from side to side being sure that no one was paying attention to their conversation. Her voice was barely audible when she spoke.

"I don't know how true this information is, but from what I understand, the Elders are planning a starve-out for the Outsiders to try and thin out the population. I overheard Jasper whispering it to a couple of his friends as they passed by, but I don't know how true it is or what it fully entails. I just wanted to let you and your family know in case it turns out to be true. It's just awful what they want to do and how they treat you just for being Outsiders. It just isn't fair, and it isn't right."

Tears were pooling in her eyes. Lance couldn't help but give her a hug. "Thank you," he whispered while still hugging her tightly, "I'll make sure this information gets to my family. We'll be alright and everything will be okay. Now we can prepare ourselves."

She hugged him back with a sniffle. She pulled away and wiped her face away quickly. "Okay," she said, "Go visit my son. He misses you."

Lance nodded with a smile. "Okay, I'll get down there right away! I'll see you soon, Beatrice!"

Lance quickly made his way to the basement, traveling on muscle memory as his mind was preoccupied with Beatrice's words causing a tight knot to form in his gut. This was the last thing that his family needed.

The basement of the Alabaster Rampart was where the indoor gardening operation was. There were two rooms: the generator room and the grow room.

The generator room was mainly comprised of about twenty or so exercise bikes hooked up to the main generator that provided electricity for the entirety of the Alabaster Rampart that were continually manned around the clock by rotating teams of operators. That power then fed into lights that were hanging inside of the grow room along with the exhaust fans, and from there into the rest of the building. In the Old World, the asylum had installed a massive indoor greenhouse for some of the patients as a therapeutic activity. Luckily for the Community when the structure was repurposed for them the grow room was restocked with soil, seeds, and other mechanical supplies for it to continue running, though lately it seemed to be on its last legs as lately the plants weren't yielding any food, and when they did, their size was less than impressive. Not to mention the poor state of the tools which resembled old relics more than shovels, rakes, and hoes.

Lance had attempted to both be a grower and a member of the generator team in the past, but they weren't for him. There was only so much reading and plant-picking he could do before he felt like he was going insane from boredom. It just wasn't stimulating enough for him like being out in the woods.

His mother knew he was meant to be a hunter from the very beginning. It was in his attitude, his body, and his eyes, but he didn't want to bring harm to any of the animals out in the surrounding forest. He would see what they looked like when his mother would bring them back to be prepared, and for years he would cry until one day at the age of twelve he was able to tolerate seeing their limp bodies. From there, his mother brought him along into the woods for hunting lessons.

In fact, the first time he ever saw a dead animal was when he was four years old. His mother had just come back from a hunt when Lance was returning home from school. He ran up to his mother without noticing the gaggle of stiff rodents hanging from her belt. It wasn't until he was a few feet from her with his arms outstretched that he saw them and turned away immediately crying and running back to the cabin. For three days he couldn't look his mother in the eye without seeing the string of animals dangling from her waist, their dried blood crusting their fur from where his mother's arrows had found their mark.

It wasn't until he was seventeen years old that he finally went into the woods with his mother as a full-fledged hunter after quitting his role as a grower and as a generator runner. He found out just how peaceful it was to trek around the woods, listening to the birds, seeing the different plants, and getting away from all the noise back home. Once was far enough into the woods, the only thing he could hear was the natural noise of the forest instead of the hustle and bustling noise of home that seemed to go on without ever stopping.

When he finally entered the grow room, he saw his father hunched over a plant. He had a magnifying glass strapped to his head and he was gently fussing over a brown and wilted pepper plant that didn't look like it wouldn't make it through the night. Lance approached slowly and silently. When he was close enough to reach out, he drove two fingers into each of his father's sides yelling, "Hi, Dad!" Marick yelped and turned around. His face was red, and his eyes were wide with a mixture of fright and anger.

"Dammit, Lance," he laughed when he realized it was his son, "What are you doing down here?"

"I came by to see Wallais. I saw you and figured I'd pop in and say 'Hi.'"

"You damn near gave me a heart attack."

"Sorry."

They both grinned like children. Lance wasn't really sorry and his father wasn't really mad. This was just one of their ways of having fun together to help pass the time. His father would only get him back later when he wasn't paying attention, as would he afterward in the never-ending cycle. Shushannah found it annoying, but they didn't care and carried on. It was important to them. A little laughter can go a long way, especially in tough times which seemed to be the norm as of late.

Once, Marick thought it would be funny to try and include her in the joke and only wound up with a broken nose. He snuck up behind her while she was washing her face for the day and drove his fingers into her sides and yelled, "Hello!" Before he could react, she turned around and swung as her reflexes kicked in before she could realize what was happening, her fist connecting with the center of his face, knocking Marick onto his ass. It was enough for Lance to know they wouldn't be playing this with her again.

From that point on, Lance and his father thought it was safer for their well-being to not mess with Shushannah.

"Hey, Dad, on a more serious note, I have to talk to you and Mom tonight about something. Beatrice shared some bad news with me that you two should know."

The smile fell from his father's face. "I think I already know. I spoke with Wallais earlier, but yes, we need to talk about it and get a plan together just in case."

"Glad we're on the same page. I'll see you later. I'm going to see Wallais."

"Alright. See you later, buddy."

Lance stared in disbelief as he weaved through the grow tables housing mostly wilted plants. The sight of them made him feel sick to his stomach, he hadn't realized just how bad things were looking down here. Some of the leaves were withered and colorless, while the other plants that were strong enough to grow food only had small, sad looking vegetable or berries that could barely be considered a snack for a toddler. The soil in their containers was moist, but the nutrients had been completely sucked out of the dirt over the years, making the soil as effective as sand. This was not a good omen of things to come—especially with the cold months around the corner where animals were even harder to come across.

When Lance finally found Wallais, he too was standing over a plant of his own with a frown. It was long dead and would not be returning to life. Its body was the same color of the dirt it was planted in and there was no support in its stalk. He was poking away at the stem with a pencil, hopeful to try and get it to stand up, only to have it flop back over uselessly.

"You should wear a mask, I think the poor thing died from being stuck looking at your face all day," Lance teased at his friend.

"Huh?" Wallais looked up and smiled, "Fuck you. You're probably cursing the place with your smell you dirty Outsider. C'mere!"

The boys laughed as they embraced. Wallais had been Lance's best friend for as long as he could remember. They were born in the same year so they grew up together. They attended the same classes, played, ate dinner, and even explored the compound when they were allowed out of the front of Lance's house. They were completely inseparable from one another.

"How's it going?" Lance asked as they stepped away from each other.

"Well, I unfortunately killed this thing, but I do have to say it lived longer than I expected."

"What was that for? Three days?"

"No, four."

They laughed again, but the light from his friend's eyes soon faded when they again rested on the dead plant in front of them. They laughed, but they knew the situation was only going to get worse and something would need to be done and soon.

"We should grab some stew together tonight. A little birdie told me there was some deer in it," Lance said with a wink, trying to brighten his friend's mood a bit.

"No way! For real? About time! I was tired of slurping down that gray water Gordin calls soup. We won't be getting much more produce from the plants this year."

"Well, with you tending to them it's no surprise to me!"

"At least I'm not scaring off all our food," Wallais jokingly retorted.

"Hey, who just brought some food back for us tonight?"

"Alright, alright, you got me. You're on for tonight, dude. I'll meet you after the dinner bell goes off at the front doors of the canteen."

"Sounds good. I'll see you. I have to meet up with my parents first but I'll be there."

They bumped fists before Lance took off back upstairs. He bolted back to his house to drop off his things before dinner, eager to taste the meat he and his mother had brought back. Shushannah and Adelade were already waiting inside as expected once he got home. Adelade was drawing a picture at the table while Shushannah washed the dried mud from her face.

"Back already?" she asked through water splashes.

"Yeah. I'm meeting Wallais for dinner later on. I wanted to come back and get cleaned up."

He stripped his bow and quiver and put it against the wall near Shushannah's. He waited his turn to use the wash basin, which was now full of muddied water. He was able to use it to clean himself up enough before dumping it out to be replaced later on. Once he was done, he placed a kiss on top of Adelade's head. She didn't notice as she was too concerned with her drawing to notice anything going on around her. He kicked off his boots and went to his "room", though it was more of a section than a room. He had some tattered sheets to block off his bed, a table, a chair, and a small dresser that held three outfits in total. He stripped his leather hunting clothes off and pulled on his usual casual wear: patched pants and a sweater.

He sat down next to Adelade once he was all done and looked at the mixed colors on the page in front of her.

"What are you drawing?" he asked.

"A monkey."

To Lance it looked more like a mess of scribbles, but he shrugged it off and played along.

"Good job," he lied enthusiastically.

He learned it from his parents who without a doubt learned it from their own parents and so on and so forth. He found it to be very useful when he didn't know what else to say to his sister, who thankfully hadn't yet caught on to the trick, or if she did, she didn't let it show.

Lance's leg started to bounce as his thoughts trailed away from the monkey and back to about what Beatrice told him earlier. He had to hope to himself that it was just gossip, but there was a part of him deep down that knew it wouldn't be a surprise if it came true. The Elders favored the Founders as that is where they originally came from. The Outsiders were only a liability at this point since they were just the run-off population.

"What's wrong?" Adelade asked, interrupting his train of thought. She was looking up at him with concerned eyes the color of a deep cerulean Summer sky.

"Nothing, kiddo. I'm alright."

She smiled up at him, believing his lie before returning to her picture. He wished he could be her age again. It was a wonderful thing to be ignorant to the problems of the world. He sighed and watched her color her picture instead and again zoned out.

The front door, and only door, to their house opened to reveal Marick, Seamus and Ogden. Marick had dirt and leaves stuck to him like always, no doubt from sifting through the rest of the dead plants in the growing room, while the other two were clean with excited smiles.

Ogden nearly flung Marick to the ground as he bulldozed his way into the house after Lance.

"You did great today, Little One!" Lance was standing up now, bracing himself. Ogden pulled him into a tight bear-hug that suffocated him to the point of unconsciousness. When he was finally let go, his head swam as the blood rushed back and the black spots dissipated from his vision. Lance adjusted himself with a nervous laugh. Then he made an *oof,* sound as Ogden's meaty hand slapped his right shoulder.

Shushannah, Seamus, and Marick were all laughing. Adelade was the only one frowning. "Don't hit my brother," she yelled with a tiny finger pointing up at Ogden. He laughed warm and heartily. He knelt, his long,bushy beard nearly touching the floor. "I'm sorry, Princess. I won't do it again, okay?"

"You better not," she chastised, "He's very frail."

Everyone laughed even harder, even Lance despite the comment being made as his expense. Adelade pouted, angry because she was the only one not laughing, not aware of what was so funny. She puffed her cheeks, grabbed her drawings, and stormed off to her "room", which was more of a sectioned off area with curtains. She whipped the sheet closed and dropped her belongings on the wood floor with a clatter.

The laughter had quieted down to muffled snorts. Lance's stomach began to growl. "Did you two just come from Gordin's kitchen?"

"Yeah. The food is just about done. We figured we would come give you our congrats on the deer, dude. Nice bag," Seamus congratulated, bumping Lance's fist.

"Good. I'm starved. Shall we all head out together?" Marick suggested.

He was dabbing his now clean face with a towel. His hands were still crusted over with dirt that had settled into his fingernail beds and the cracks of his hands. Lance couldn't remember a time when his father's hands *weren't* dirty. It was as if the dirt and his skin had become one.

"I guess I could eat," Adelade's muffled voice said behind her curtain. Ogden chuckled and pulled the curtain back revealing Adelade who didn't appear angry anymore.

"I'm meeting up with Wallais, but I can walk with you all to the canteen," Lance noted.

"Then let's go, I'm about to keel over," Shushannah remarked.

She rose from her chair and paraded out of the house. The troupe followed her in a straight line through the compound and up to the front door of the Alabaster Rampart. They marched through to the giant mess hall in the back right next to Gordin's kitchen. There was a serving station that he and a few others were manning. Soup was being ladled into bowls like always, but tonight it smelled better than ever. Lance couldn't tell if it was because there was meat and spices now added to the stew or if it was because he was starving, either way he wanted a heaping portion of it. His mouth was watering before he was even able to grab his bowl. He could see Wallais in line waving at him. He hadn't yet gotten his soup. Lance waved back and resumed his spot in line. He would meet up with him after.

"I'm glad you two are friends," Ogden told Lance. There was a light pat on his shoulder this time. It was affectionate and much more well received. "I think this whole 'Founders' and 'Outsiders' thing is bullshit. We're all struggling to survive out here and all people can do is think of ways to tear each other apart. It makes you wonder, is this really the fate of humanity? Are we doomed to repeat what our ancestors did? You two are breaking the mold. I mean, we all are really, but you two especially. I wish more people could see that we would get by together instead of divided and bickering with each other all day."

"Thanks, Ogden. That means a lot. I'm glad we're friends too—all of us. I wouldn't want it any other way."

Ogden pulled Lance in for another bear-hug.

The line moved rather fast to Lance's approval as he moved closer and closer to the steaming pot that Gordin was ladling soup from.

"Hey, Gordin," he greeted his happy little friend behind the counter.

"The man of the hour! The soup is a hit! I had enough meat to feed an army from that thing! These people have warm, wholesome food in their bellies because of *you*!" Shushannah audibly cleared her throat in front of Lance. "And your mother too!"

"That's better. Don't you forget it," she threw back with a grin.

Lance collected his soup and bid his friends and family goodbye as he trotted off to join Wallais at the table he picked.

"Hey, what's up?" he said as he took a seat across from his friend.

"Since, like, an hour ago? I solved the hunger crisis, got married, had three kids and then got divorced."

"Wow, so you've done nothing?"

"Yup."

"Thought so."

"But on a more serious note, I think we need to test the soil outside again. The stuff we're using just isn't cutting it anymore. We're losing more plants than are producing."

"I think so too. Maybe we'll get better results from another test. Has anyone told you if they'll be going out to do another soon?"

Wallais shook his head. "No, but I think I'll—," he was cut off when a bowl of hot broth collided with the side of his head. Steam started to waft from his already reddening skin as he hurriedly wiped the scalding liquid from his face with his sleeve.

"What are you doing sitting with an Outsider? You want to join them? You want to roll around in the filth with those dirt dwellers?" a man's voice hollered from down the end of their table.

Wallais had tears in his eyes that were either due to the hot soup or the insults. Either way, Lance wasn't about to stand for that. "Why don't you say what you said to my face then, asshole, then you can see what happens when you roll around with a 'dirt-dweller.'"

The soup assailants were a group of three men that Lance recognized as the maintenance team responsible for keeping the Alabaster Rampart in working order though he didn't know any of them by name. They were still in their matching yellow overalls, obviously either on break or just recently done for the day. Lance assumed the man standing up and shooting him a nasty glare was the one responsible for hurling insults and wasting good food. He was about the same height as Lance though he didn't have the same muscle tone. Under his greasy blonde hair the man was sneering back at him. "What did you say to me? You filthy fucking dirt ball?"

Lance gritted his teeth, stood up and slowly walked towards the three men. His heart was racing in his chest. His brain was telling him to turn and run, but his rage—his mother's uncontrollable rage—was telling him to dump his stew right over their heads and teach them a lesson.

"I said: 'Why don't you say it to my face then, *asshole*!'"

His tongue felt numb in his mouth as he continued forwards, his pace quickening, propelled by dizzying rage and adrenaline. The three men looked at each other with eager grins and began their descent on Lance expecting an easy fight. Lance kept himself steady as his hunting instincts kicked in. His senses began to heighten and became spatially aware of his surroundings. He stood still as the three men surrounded him and waited for them to stop moving.

The room was silent as all eyes watched intently to see what was going to happen next. The guards would for sure intervene, but not before some blood was spilled. They wanted a show just as much as the rest of the people around here.

The blonde man charged forward first with a roar and his stomach swaying back and forth from the inertia. Lance side-stepped and planted a palm square on his back, sending him sprawling over the empty table between them and Wallais. He didn't have time to dodge the next man that drove a hard fist into the right side of Lance's face. He felt the impact but no pain, not yet. He fired a fist back but missed. His attacker's friend tackled Lance and pinned him to the ground.

"Filthy outsider," the other spat as he kicked Lance in the side repeatedly. He could feel that and knew he would *really* feel it in the morning. The air was knocked out of him with every blow. He couldn't wriggle out of the hands of his captor and the repeated kicks were clouding his thoughts as all he could think of was how much it hurt. His panic grew as he realized there was no escape from the man's grasp and the swinging foot.

He didn't have to struggle much longer though as a boot belonging to Wallais shot straight into the man's face that was pinning down Lance. Blood dropped from his mouth and nose onto Lance's face as the man fell backwards. Lance jumped up, holding his side but still looking to keep fighting. He wiped the blood, smearing it across his face and staining his sleeve.

Wallais was now struggling with the blonde man and the one who was kicking Lance's sides. Lance grabbed the one who was kicking him and yanked him back hard onto the tile floor. He drove a fist into the man's face three times before he was pulled off.

"You son of a bitch," he roared, "I'll knock your fucking teeth in!"

He was yanked backwards and pinned down by multiple hands.

"Shit," he cursed.

He stopped struggling and looked at the faces of the guards leering down at him. He stopped struggling and allowed them to pick him up and escort him from the canteen. He had an inkling of what would happen next but he still didn't regret his actions. He knew he was going to the offices at the top level to be put in front of the Elders for judgement. Whether or not the others would be in trouble he was unsure of. Being "Founders" they would probably get a slap on the wrist while the "Outsider" would most likely bear the brunt of the punishment though he was only defending himself and a fellow "Founder".

Whatever.

As he left the canteen he saw the faces of his parents, Adelade, Ogden, Seamus, and Beatrice. They all had their mouths hanging open except for Shushannah who looked as if she was ready to dump her soup over Lance's head. *Never give the Founders a reason to hate us more, no matter what,* his mother's words echoed in his head.

He was paraded through the empty hallways of the Rampart, up flights of stairs and then stopped in front of the offices that he was always told to never, ever go into unless otherwise instructed. He swallowed down a hard lump that had formed in his throat. He could feel his body shaking as the last of his adrenaline was wearing off and being replaced by nerves.

He had never been in serious trouble before and didn't fully know what would happen to him or what to expect when he went into the room. As a child for fighting, he only received detention which was typically writing lines until his hand cramped up, or more recently, being put on dishes duty. He'd seen adults get in trouble, and that they were forced to do some of the more... obscene jobs that the Community was normally responsible for.

In his entire life, he only knew of one execution, but that was for murder at least 10 years ago. He obviously wasn't going to die for a little spat like this, but he was sure that he would be getting a very dehumanizing punishment that would make him wish he was being executed.

He was pushed into the room and forced into a chair.

It was dimly lit with a bright red carpet on the white marble floor. The chair in which he was seated was more comfortable than he expected, though not by much. It was wooden with a cracked pleather seat. Sitting across from him were the three Elders of the Community with their hands crossed over the surface of a glossy, wooden desk.

"Caught this one, Wallais from the gardens and the maintenance crew fighting in the canteen. We separated the others out to cool down for a while. We will bring them in after."

"Thank you, Alan. We can take it from here."

The guard left the room, leaving Lance alone with the Elders.

The three Elders in their usual black robes steadily stared at Lance. They had empty bowls in front of them. They obviously enjoyed the deer that Lance had taken down earlier that day, but he doubted that it would not help him get in their good graces.

Jasper's father, Elder Maxwell, sat off to Lance's left. He had long dark hair and the same ever-present scowl cemented on his face. Lance figured he always had a stick up his ass because he wanted to be the head Elder. Everybody knew it, but he was far from being where he wanted to. He was only recently put into power about five years ago when Elder Caleb passed away from old age and Maxwell was brought in.

The head Elder, Elder Sampson, was completely bald. He had a soft yet intimidating face. He was the one that always spoke for the trio. His voice always sounded gravely as long as Lance had been alive. He was tall and skinny, and he always walked around with his hood up and hands interlaced behind his back. He was old and would soon be stepping down from the council as did most Elders where he would then be doted on hand and foot for the service he provided to the Community. Despite his age, he always moved around the Rampart with unexpected grace and speed.

On the right was Elder Borris. He was the next in line for command of the Elders despite what Elder Maxwell wanted. He was fairer than the others, but not by much. He was one of the heavier-set people of the Community. He was a man that loved to indulge when he could. Lance assumed the food issue would impact Borris the most, but he doubted that he would miss a meal himself unless it was extremely dire circumstances. He had long hair and a scraggly beard. He looked as if he had been satisfied by the soup tonight as he kept stealing glances down at the bowl to see if there were any morsels he missed when he sucked it down.

"What are we to do with you, boy?" Maxwell snarled. Sampson stopped him with a mere raise of his hand. Maxwell's head slumped like a scolded puppy. Lance couldn't help but pity him. Even in a place of power he had no power. What a miserable existence.

"We will hear his story first, Maxwell. I'm sure Lance has a good reason for starting a brawl in the middle of dinner. Let's hear it."

Lance cleared his throat, very surprised by Sampson's reaction. Maybe it wouldn't be so bad after all.

"The three men that my friend and I were fighting with threw a bowl of hot soup at my friend. They were berating us for being friends since I am an 'Outsider' and he is a 'Founder'. He was upset, as was I, so I retaliated. The three men attacked first, and I just defended myself. My friend joined in when the men pinned me down and repeatedly kicked me in the side. I'm sorry that we caused all of that, but I couldn't just let them insult me and my friend."

"We will hear the story from your friend as well as our workers. As of right now we can't allow this transgression to go unpunished. After you finish your hunting rounds, we expect you to report to the sanitation department. For two weeks you will clean the latrines within the Alabaster Rampart. After the completion of your two weeks, you will be forgiven for your lapse of judgement."

"Thank you, Sirs. I promise, this won't happen again."

"You are dismissed," Sampson granted with a wave of his hand.

Lance scurried out of the room as fast as he could. His heart was still beating a hundred miles an hour. He hoped things would go well for Wallais. He was sure that it would though considering the importance of Wallais's role in the Community and that he was from a Founder Family.

Dinner would be well over by now. He would have to wait until tomorrow to eat most likely. Damn. He was looking forward to eating the soup tonight too. Nobody would have taken him any food as it wasn't allowed out of the mess hall. He was sure his parents were just as pissed at him as the Elders. He held his fluttering stomach that was in pain both from the kicking and from not being able to eat. He wasn't out of the frying pan just yet.

Night had settled faster over the compound than he had hoped. The stars twinkled through the windows of the Rampart as he raced back home.

To his disapproval, he realized once he got outside that the temperature had plummeted. He shivered as he ran home wishing that he had put on a warmer sweater. Plumes of steam came from his mouth as he huffed along. It was just another thing to add to his worries. Winter was well on its way with no signs of slowing anytime soon. He hoped it would be a mild one. Snow and starvation would not be a good combination.

He pushed open the door to his house to find his parents seated at their table. Addie was lying on the floor, coloring another picture while humming a tune he didn't recognize.

"Sit," Shushannah commanded before he could step over the threshold, "We have to talk.

3

Lance had been stuck on toilet duty for a week now, but to him it felt more like a year. The palms of his hands were sore and beginning to blister from all the scrubbing. He didn't realize just how disgusting the Founders could be until he was on his hands and knees scrubbing fecal matter from the grouted tile of their restrooms.

How it got there he didn't know, nor did he want to know. He struggled to keep vomit down as he worked. He doubted much would come up anyways, but he didn't want to clean more than he already had to. His time in the various bathrooms within the Alabaster Rampart made him realize that he preferred the outdoor toilet he used to the ones inside. There wasn't much privacy—spare the particle board dividers between the toilets. Although, on the other hand, there was still working plumbing inside of the Alabaster Rampart, unlike Lance's home where they used a bucket in a separate room behind their little cabin.

The same generators running the growing room helped to power the built-in plumbing system that had been installed back in the old world. Occasionally, he had seen some of the maintenance crew behind the massive structure trying to pump out the sewage when it was backed up. There were many things that he hadn't realized about the differences between the Founders and the Outsiders. For one, the

Alabaster Rampart was always the perfect temperature. He never felt too hot or too cold and it made him realize just how uncomfortable the air could be at times when living outside.

Then there was the electricity. The lights were always on and he never recalled seeing someone having to use a candle to struggle to read or work their way down the corridors to the bathrooms he worked so hard to clean for them lately—not to mention the fact that they could listen to music if they wanted, which was uncommon for the Outsiders unless one of the few musicians put on a show. Everything inside was pristine and comfortable, spare the bathrooms until he was finished with them. He stifled a yawn into his shoulder, not daring to open his mouth should the cleaning products get inside—or something else.

Thoughts of his cold, dimly lit cabin made him long to lay in one of the many rooms to rest his head. He remembered all the times he stayed over Wallais's over the years and how much more comfortable they were than sleeping on a bundle of blankets on the floor where they would be forced to brush bugs off of themselves throughout the night. It really set the line between civilized living and savage living. He stifled another yawn, thinking that he would even sleep here on the dingy, disgusting tile flooring if he could. He grinned to himself remembering that he had only one more week left of cleaning and then he could relax after a long day of tracking through the woods instead of having to do this shit. He just hoped he could get *through* the week. He found himself falling asleep on tree branches or in bushes during the day while he waited for something to come by. Shushannah angrily woke him up two days ago when he slept through his entire shift by pushing him off a branch. He landed on the hard dirt below, disoriented. She was pissed.

"Nice to know you have time to nap while I bust my ass trying to bring some food home," she snarled. She shot him dirty looks the entirety of the night when he returned from his sanitation shift. He ignored them, but he could feel her eyes digging into him, even when he drew his curtain to go to sleep, he could tell she was staring at him through the tattered fabric.

To add to his sleeping issues, he continually reflected on the conversation he had with his parents the night he came back from the Elders' Chamber after receiving his punishment. Evidently, Beatrice had told everyone at dinner that night before the fight broke out about what she heard Jasper talking about, but that she wasn't sure if it was something that could be trusted, though the last part fell on deaf ears. His mother only heard what she wanted to hear. Shushannah pointed a finger at Lance later that same night when he returned home and told him that his actions in the mess hall had given a reason to the Elders to starve the Outsiders. He knew she was only trying to cast blame from her own anxieties, so he didn't take it to heart, but it still didn't stop him from feeling upset with her over it.

They stayed up most of that night trying to figure out what they would do if the Elders said they were going to enact this "solution". They couldn't very well just leave since there wasn't anything out there for them, not to mention they had Adelade to think of and she wouldn't be able to last very long out in the woods.

The forest wasn't that big surrounding the Community and they would surely be found, and if it was Jasper to find them, he was sure that it would spell nothing but trouble for them. In the end, there wasn't anything they could do except to wait and see if the rumors were true, and if they were, to just ride out the storm and hope for the best. Not having an answer weighed heavily on them, creating an anxious tension in the air. Even Adelade was beginning to pick up on it too. It was moments like that where Lance found his mind wondering if it were possible for the Elders to be lying to them all about the Edge. What proof did they *really* have that it was dangerous out there besides losing contact with the other Communities?

There were never any teams sent out to see if their stories were true. So how did they know that for sure? Lance never dared to go past the Edge to seek out the truth himself, nor did any of the other hunters to the best of his knowledge. He figured that Jasper may have, but if he did, it wouldn't make much sense for him to say anything to anyone because his father was an Elder, and with that sort of power already in his possession, why would he want to throw it away and expose their lies? Of course, again, that is if he even *did* venture beyond the Edge.

He felt as if he were drowning with nothing to pull himself free from the water. Everything was collapsing in on him. He slammed the mop into the brown water, splashing himself slightly in the process with the murky water, but he paid it no mind. He closed his eyes, rubbing the bridge of his nose, and tried to calm his anxieties by slowly taking in air into his tightened chest. He eventually returned to mopping, not wanting someone to wander into the restroom to find him just standing around. If word got back to the Elders that he wasn't performing his punishment, he could kiss that light at the end of the tunnel goodbye. There was a noise in the distance that jolted him from his thoughts and back to reality with a slight twitch. His stomach dropped when he heard the sound of approaching voices. He silently prayed to himself that it wasn't Jasper as the footsteps came closer. He couldn't handle a berating from him right now. He realized it wasn't when he could hear the deep voice clearer as whoever it was grew closer, but there was still something about the voice that seemed familiar enough to keep his stomach twisting. He bowed his head and aimlessly dragged his mop over the tile, being sure to turn his back on the entrance to the restroom as the door was pushed open, bringing a few males into the room. He pushed around the small puddle at his feet, his ears perking up to listen to the conversation much like they do when he hears the snapping of a twig while out in the woods.

"Yeah, I wasn't shocked that they didn't even pull me into their chambers. Why would they punish one of their own? Besides, it was that little bastard Outsider that really caused a problem. He shouldn't be hanging around with one of ours, it's just not right. I just wish the guards hadn't stepped in when they did, I would've given that little shit something to remember."

"I bet, Tim," another voice chimed in, "I bet you would've given him a good thumping!"

Lance recognized the voice almost immediately—his veins turning to ice, almost wishing that it was Jasper that had walked into the bathroom instead. His tongue sat uncomfortably in his mouth as adrenaline began to slowly pump into his system and he kept his gaze downward. He was sure that it was the same guy he got into a fight with last week that put him in his current predicament. His chest fluttered madly as he kept working, slowly inching away to the back corner of the bathroom where he hoped he would just blend in with the background.

He dared to steal a peek over his shoulder, and just with his luck, there was the man from before, still sporting a black eye. His lip wasn't swollen anymore, but there was still the faint outline of a healing cut from where it split open.

"Well, well, well," Tim clucked when he saw Lance, "Look who it is, boys." He strode towards Lance as if he were royalty with two other men trailing behind him that Lance did not recognize. The three men surrounded him, backing him into a corner. Both men on either side of Timothy towered over Lance, but they weren't as lean, both sporting bellies showing that they eat more than they work—a curious thing given the Community's current predicament. They clearly weren't missing any meals.

Tim stopped, looking Lance up and down with a smirk. "I see they put you where you belong—with the shit." he sneered, but he didn't look very intimidating with his still healing eye. He looked more like a wounded playground bully still trying to flex whatever meager amount of power he had. "I think you missed a spot over here."

Lance watched as Tim turned his back and heard the fly of his zipper come down. A second later, a yellow stream splattered on the tile that Lance had been mopping not ten minutes before. He gripped the mop, wondering what it would feel like to break it over the back of Tim's head, but he reeled himself in. He sunk his teeth into his tongue, drawing a slight copper taste as he punctured the top layer of flesh and waited for the splatter to turn into small droplets. Tim pulled his zipper up and turned on his heel with a cheeky grin. "C'mon boys, we're done here."

The trio left the bathroom, laughing to themselves loudly, proud of what they had done. Hearing the words coming out of Tim's mouth that he hadn't gotten so much as a slap on the wrist was sadly no surprise to Lance. Tim was a Founder, and Founders looked after their own after all. He slammed the mop into the bucket again and slapped it hard into the puddle of urine that had now settled into the grout of the tile. He did his best to try and clean it up, though it was just being pushed around more and more with the acrid smell threatening to turn his stomach inside out. He clenched his teeth, white knuckling the handle in his hands, whipping the mop back and forth. He was defending his friend—defending himself—but yet he was the one in trouble cleaning up the urine from the asshole that *should* be the one pushing piss and shit around all day.

He huffed angrily as a searing fire surged through is body and tossed the mop to the side hissing, "Fuck this."

He flung open the door, bouncing it loudly off of the rubber doorstop and stomped down the hallway towards the Chamber of the Elders, his boots squeaking every step, wet from the mixture of piss and mop water. His mother's temper was once again guiding his body and clouding all rational thought. The only thing on his mind was tearing the Elders a new asshole and telling them where they could stick their punishment. He was running on autopilot as his mind was focused on piecing together the speech that would ultimately put him on cleaning duty the entirety of his remaining living years, that or would result in his public execution. It wasn't until he turned the corner and walked right into the solid wall of Ogden's body that his mind finally pumped the brakes and began to come back to its senses.

Lance fell back, looking up at the grinning wall of a man. A lump formed in Lance's throat as Ogden hauled him up with one hand and then clapped him hard on his right shoulder, sending the remnants of his rage into oblivion. He suddenly wished he was back cleaning up piss. "Hey little one," Ogden boomed, "Where are you off to in such a hurry?"

Lance couldn't get the words to come out of his mouth. It was for the best that he didn't confess his true intentions. "Uh, I was going to head home," he lied, "I'm done with my sanitation shift for the night."

"I'll join you," Ogden happily obliged, pulling Lance into the opposite direction, the right direction towards the exit, with little to no effort.

Lance was about to take it upon himself to end his shift for the night anyways. After the urine incident, he had enough for the night. As long as the bathroom on this floor had the appearance of being cleaned he would be fine. He had pushed the urine around enough that nobody would be able to tell that the floor wasn't really clean, unless they really wanted to get up close and personal with the piss puddle and smell it. The pair descended the front stairwell to the lobby entrance, which was practically empty now as it was the end of the day, and walked into the brisk autumn night. The moon was casting silver pools of light through the overgrown trees as they crossed the field towards Lance's house.

"I know where you were going," Ogden whispered, catching Lance off-guard.

"What?"

"I know where you were going. You were going to the Chamber of the Elders. It's a good thing I caught you. You were about to condemn yourself. What was going through your head?"

Lance couldn't help but feel ashamed of his actions.

The tone in Ogden's voice was one of disappointment, and it was a tone that he seldom heard. Despite his roughness, Ogden was a man that he looked up to his whole life, and to disappoint him like this made him feel sick. "That guy, Tim, he got off without so much as a slap on the wrist. I heard him bragging about it. He started the whole fight, but yet *I'm* the one that gets in trouble. He pissed all over the bathroom floor just to rub it in my face. I was going to tell the Elders off for picking sides."

A puff of steam erupted from Ogden's flat nose sitting just above his bushy mustache. "I hear what you're saying, Lance. I agree, it isn't fair, but you won't change anything going around letting your temper do the talking for you. Tim will get what he deserves, in fact you already gave it to him. He has to walk around sporting that black eye and split lip for what he did, and there's nothing more embarrassing than that."

Lance could tell that this was about to turn into a speech that he had to sit through with his dad as a kid at the age of nine when he got into his first fight with Jasper. It was the "be the bigger man" speech. He hated that speech.

"Fuck that," he breathed, "They shouldn't be playing favorites! They should be making fair decisions! You should be mad too for what they did to Wallais!"

"You think I am not mad? I'm furious, but it is as I said before, Tim will get what he deserves. It won't be any good to get all of us in trouble for the ignorance of one person."

"Well, I still think Tim should have gotten more. In fact, I feel like the Elders only punished me because I'm an Outsider and not because of the fight. If I was a Founder I bet things would have been different, and I know *you* know that deep down, Ogden. I was the only one—*the only one*—that got punished that night. And it's not just Tim, it's all the Founders—no offense. All the Founders are treated differently. Any moron can see it."

Ogden was silent. Lance was surprised, but he didn't dwell on it. He was too furious to think of anything else other than being wronged. The Elders were only looking out for themselves and their "people". Things aren't ever going to change. He was the shit under their heels and nothing more no matter how much smoke they blew up his ass about being a good hunter. It was all bullshit, he thought to himself.

They reached Lance's home finally after a long silence that was uncharacteristically like Ogden. "Would you like to come in?" Lance asked as cheerily as he could.

"Not tonight, Little One. I just wanted to be sure you got home safe without making any unwise decisions. Wish everyone a good night for me, okay?"

"You got it. Thank you again, Ogden. You and your family are some of the good ones."

Ogden smiled and turned to head back to the Alabaster Rampart.

On some level, the more rational level of Lance's mind, he was thankful. No good would have come from him barging in on the Elders and yelling at them like he was planning. He was happy that Ogden was watching out for him and his family, but there was still an unsatisfied itch that he didn't scratch that made him twist uncomfortably in his clothing.

He waited a moment before entering his home. Some part of him wanted to sneak in and finish what he started, but yet again, the rational side won over and he retired to his home, eager to see his family.

Marick and Shushannah were sitting at the table by a flickering candle. Lance could hear the soft snoring of Adelade behind her curtain. He hadn't been aware of just how late it was. All he wanted to do was climb into bed and forget the day.

"How was sanitation duty tonight?" Marick asked as Lance washed his hands thoroughly. No amount of scrubbing ever made him feel clean after cleaning the bathrooms. It would be a while before he could move past the feeling.

"Shitty."

Marick scoffed while Shushannah's scowled remained unwavering. She was still annoyed with Lance from the other day. He ignored her and assumed it would just blow over like always. Besides, he was too exhausted to care.

"I saw that guy from the fight last week tonight, Tim," Lance stated flatly as he took a seat at the table. Both Marick and Shushannah looked at him, worried expressions plastered on both of their faces.

Lance put up a hand. "I'm fine. He was still upset about things, but he didn't start anything. He did mention something that pissed me off though."

Shushannah leaned in. Lance knew her intuition already knew what was going to come out of his mouth.

"He was bragging about not getting punished for the fight," she said for him.

Shushannah's face turned tomato red when Lance nodded and her fist balled up tightly, turning the flesh on her knuckles white. She looked as if she were about to explode. Both Marick and Lance exchanged glances of nervousness, hoping that Adelade wouldn't be awoken by Shushannah's building outburst.

"He came into the bathroom I was cleaning, and I heard him bragging to a couple of other guys he was with that he didn't even get so much as a slap on the wrist," he explained.

"Those Elders are assholes," she snarled, "They're just as bad as Tim. They're going to cause a goddamned war pulling shit like this."

Lance knew that the divide between the Founders and the Outsiders grew wider day by day. Tensions were high and he knew something was going to happen sooner or later. This was just another thing added to an already long, and still growing, list. Now they were openly choosing the side of the Founders rather than looking after the Community as a whole. That meant they couldn't be trusted, and as history dictates, nothing good comes from a leader that cannot be trusted, especially when things were crumbling around them. It was only a matter of time before the pedestal the Elders had placed themselves on collapsed from underneath them.

"I didn't want to say anything before," Marick muttered, "But I have heard talk of rebellion from some of the others around here. They're losing faith in the Elders to get us through this food crisis."

Shushannah's head snapped around to him so fast that Lance thought that she may accidentally break it. "Why didn't you say anything?" she demanded.

Lance could see a fire burning in her eyes. It was as if she was waiting for this.

"I-I didn't want to add to the gossip. It was only talk, there was no planning in place or anything like that. I thought it was just small talk, but thinking about it now makes me think there's more weight to it than I originally thought." Marick rubbed the stubble on his chin. He stared blankly at the dancing candle flame.

Shushannah didn't comment any further, but both men knew the gears were turning in her mind. Lance knew the real reason his father didn't say anything was because he knew Shushannah would see it as an option to join those willing to start a war with the Founders. She hated how things were being run and she was the type to actually drive people to act on their words. Now that it was out in the open, the pot was being stirred. He just hoped that his mother be rational about this whole thing.

Lance added that to his mental list with a sigh.

"You better get some sleep," she told Lance behind a darkened scowl, "We have an early morning tomorrow."

"I know, don't remind me," he groaned.

Lance meandered off to his area and drew his curtains around him. His head had barely hit the pillow when he finally let his exhaustion consume him. He slept heavily with no dreams and was woken roughly by his mother early the next morning. He reluctantly got up, feeling as if he had just closed his eyes and not an ounce refreshed. He splashed some water on his face and sluggishly joined his mother for their trek out to the woods. He managed to stay awake throughout the day, trying to focus his senses on the sights, sounds, and smells that the forest had to offer him, though it didn't help him much. There was still some life left in the woods though the leaves had turned to the filthy color of mud, signaling the end of warm weather and the approach of the cold, gray weather. He and his mother returned that afternoon to the Community empty handed, which only added to his discouragement. His mind was focused on the sanitation duty he would be responsible for the second he dropped off his bow and quiver.

He and Shushannah had made it no more than twenty feet back to the inner fencing when a skinny boy ran up to the pair. Lance remembered seeing him in Beatrice's classroom last year. He remembered that she called him Peter. He brushed sandy hair from his brown eyes and Lance could see that despite the brisk air, a light layer of sweat had formed on the boy's upper brow. He had no doubt been running around for quite some time. "Excuse me," he puffed, "The Elders request the presence of Lance to their chambers."

Lance sighed and rolled his eyes. He looked to his mother, and without a word, handed over his bow and quiver to follow Peter back to the Chamber of the Elders.

The whole way to their chambers, Lance hoped that the Elders would take pity on him and end his punishment early. The thought of an early night sleep made his mouth water more than a freshly cooked slice of venison. His stomach growled. He rubbed the dogging hunger pains away as he came to the now familiar door leading to the Chamber of the Elders. He walked through the door with no issue from the pair of guards on either side of the entrance and took a seat in front of the cloaked trio. He adjusted himself in his chair while the gaze of the three men lingered on him. Elder Sampson's watery eyes didn't move from Lance as if he were trying to find the correct words to say. His mouth twitched, puckering as if he were chewing on something. Lance cast his gaze downward, trying to ignore the Head Elder's stare.

The old man cleared his throat finally, making Lance jump a small amount, though if the Elders noticed, they did not react.

"Lance," Sampson began, "We called you here today to discuss your punishment. As you surely recall, we assigned you the duty of sanitation due to your actions in the mess hall a little over a week ago. The reason we assigned this role to you was to bestow upon you the grievance of your actions and how you are perceived when you act such as how you did. It is our understanding that you are upset about Timothy and the others not receiving a punishment. As it stands, you instigated the violence. Had you sat back, Timothy would have been dealt with accordingly."

Lance bit his tongue. Lies. Only lies were pouring out of Sampson's mouth.

"That being said, I have consulted with the others and we feel that you have justly served your punishment and you will no longer need to continue with sanitation duties. We feel that given your actions, that your punishment was more than lenient and we expect your behavior to change. As it was your first offense in quite some time, we felt that our initial duration was a bit much. You may be dismissed."

Despite his newfound freedom, he still felt like he was wronged. Tim getting off without so much as a dish washing chore rubbed him the wrong way. He could see Elder Maxwell glaring at him through his peripheral. Something about his look said that the decision was made by Elder Sampson to end his punishment early. Elder Borris sat calmly, unbothered with the conversation appearing to be lost in his own thoughts.

"Thank you, Sirs," Lance forced out, standing for a bow. He decided to listen to Ogden's echoing words and let the matter go. He would only stab himself in the foot if he said anything. He knew it was smarter to take the early ending to his punishment. Besides, there were more important things for him to be concerned with.

"Enjoy the rest of your night," Sampson announced with a smile.

Lance forced his face to spread into a grin, hoping that it didn't look too forced and left the Chamber of the Elders.

Walking through the halls, he watched children playing with toys instead of the sticks and pebbles most of the Outsiders used for toys growing up. One girl even had a baby doll that was much different from the straw figure that Adelade played with on occasion. Shushannah had woven it for her with pieces of twigs and branches she found out in the forest when Adelade mentioned a girl in her class had a baby doll and she wanted it. When it was presented to her, the disappointment in her face was evident, but she was still thankful for the little thatch doll. She hugged Shushannah but she only played with it on the rarest of occasions. It mostly sat in the corner of her little area collecting dust.

He sighed wondering if things would ever be different in the future. He didn't understand why there was such a huge divide in the Community. They were all struggling to survive and it made more sense to do it together rather than to alienate each other.

He tried not to think of it any further and returned to his home where he sat with his family for the duration of the night. They chatted and laughed, reminiscing about old memories as always. When the candles burned down about halfway, they all decided to turn in for the night. Lance was feeling good for the first time in a while. He held onto the feeling as he made his way to his bed.

He fluffed his blankets up as much as he could and settled in for the night. The last thought he had before closing his eyes and allowing sleep to take over, was that if given the choice, he would much rather be sleeping on the floor of his little wooden home, brushing away bugs and listening to the wind whistling outside of his open window, or dealing with the rain, because even though it made him uncomfortable, he realized that it made him who he is today and he learned to appreciate the important things in life. Comfort was meaningless if you didn't have family to share it with. No matter where he was, or what he did, he would always have his family.

They were survivors.

The people living in the Alabaster Rampart don't have the same skills he and his parents have, and if it came down to it, they wouldn't be able to do the things that he and his mother do to eat. Even though he was an Outsider, he truly was a Founder, because if it weren't for he and his family, there would be no Community: 1049.

4

Lance sat hunched over in his chair, anxiously bouncing his legs and staring at the door to his cabin. His father had been summoned to the Chamber of the Elders earlier that morning by the same sweaty little blonde-haired boy that summoned Lance nearly a week ago. Lance knew that it most likely was not good news that caused his father to be called away, but he just couldn't determine *what* the bad news could be.

His father had been absent the majority of the day now, and in that time Lance racked his brain to try and think of any transgression that his father may have committed, though he could not since his father never even so much as littered as long as he had known him.

Shushannah brought Adelade to the home of one of her friend's earlier that day to get them out of their hair for a little bit. Lance hadn't paid much attention to what Shushannah had said before she left and merely responded with a grunt while chewing on his thumb until he could taste the metallic taste of blood in his mouth. He wiped it away on his pants, leaving behind a stain that had since dried.

His mother's abrupt entrance back into the cabin derailed his train of thought, though he didn't complain as he wasn't having any luck thinking of any substantial possibilities for his father's summoning.

She uncharacteristically shuffled over to a chair and flopped down with a sigh and dropped her head onto her folded arms she had crossed on the table's surface.

"What the hell could they be talking to him about? He's been gone all damned day," she complained. Her voice came out muffled as she spoke into her arms.

"I know," Lance finally spoke. His voice came out hoarse and dry, forcing him to clear his throat. "I can't think of a single thing for them to call him for—especially something this long."

As if on cue, Marick entered the cabin, letting in a rush of freezing air with him. He stood in the doorway, shoulders slumped and his head down. He shuffled in and dropped himself into a chair. Both Lance and Shushannah's gaze bored into him, impatiently waiting for him to satisfy their burning curiosity.

After what felt like hours, Marick finally murmured, "They want us to conduct another soil test."

"That's what you were called away all day for? To be told to go out and run another soil test," Shushannah blurted with a tinge of disappointment in her voice, "They couldn't have just told you tomorrow when you went back into the grow rooms?"

"There aren't grow rooms anymore," Marick croaked.

"What? What do you mean?" Lance asked.

Marick swallowed before answering. "The Elders shut them down. There's no more nutrients in the soil and we're exhausting too much power to keep the rooms running. We've had the worst harvest in the entire history of the Community. They had the entire indoor growing staff in their chambers today. We were trying to come up with another plan, but the only way that we could continually grow would be to use the soil from the Earth instead of the used up potted soil we had been reusing for years."

"So their answer to the food crisis is to shut down the *one* place that was providing some form of food for us all? What sense does that make? Why wait until now to do something about it?" his mother questioned.

Lance had been wondering the same thing himself, especially now. *Why* hadn't the Elders tried to find a solution before now? It was like they expected everything to just work itself out.

"When do you need to go out to do the test?" Lance asked changing the subject, and curious to see how the soil test was performed.

"I go out first thing tomorrow," his father muttered.

"I'll take you," Lance volunteered quickly, "I've always wanted to see what the soil test looks like."

Marick puffed air loudly through his nose. "It isn't as glorious as it sounds. I take different soil samples and then take them back here to have them analyzed to determine if the toxins in the soil have filtered out enough to allow crops to grow in them without killing us when we consume them later."

Lance was still interested despite his father's explanation. The last time a soil test was performed was when Lance was a year younger than Adelade. They weren't done very often due to limited supplies to perform the test. It wasn't like there were still manufacturing companies open for them to buy more of their supplies. He remembered his mother and father disappeared that morning and did not return for him until later that night. He had spent the day with Wallais and his family wondering what his parents were up to. When he asked them the volley of questions he had been thinking of over the course of the day, but as they were exhausted from traveling around the forest all day, they brushed him off promising to answer his questions another time which never came.

"It's not like there's anything to hunt out in the woods lately anyways, you're more than welcome to take him. Everything has disappeared for the Winter," Shushannah complained. She stood up and stretched. "I need to get some air. I'll be back in a bit. I should get Adelade too to get her ready for bed, it's almost time to turn in for the night."

She left the two men alone in the cabin, the only noise between them was the crackling of the tiny flame eating away the wick of the candle still burning on the table casting a dancing light around the room. Marick was lost in thought, chewing the corner of his thumb. Lance wiped away a small bubble of fresh blood from his thumb on his pants, adding to his small collection of browning streaks, mimicking his father's nervous habit.

"Things aren't looking good, Lance. We're going to need to think of a solution and fast. The soil around here is still too contaminated for us to use for our crops. We need at least another decade for the pollution levels to drop, but that won't help us anyway."

"Then why do the tests? Wouldn't it just be a waste if you already know the soil isn't any good?"

His father shook his head. "You know how the Elders are. They want the test, they get the test. I just don't understand why they're putting so much into this. It's just wasting time that we already don't have."

"Don't worry, Dad. I'm sure everything will work out. If we have to, Mom and I will sneak smaller game into the house to keep some food in our bellies."

"I know we'll be fine, but I'm more concerned about the Community. We've all been so on edge lately, I think this is going to be the final nail in the coffin. If we don't fix this, the Community is surely going to collapse."

Lance sighed and began to play with the palm of his hand, running his fingertips over calluses from years of climbing and scouring against the rough bark of the trees he precariously perched himself in waiting for prey to come his way. He didn't know what to say, if there was even anything *to* say.

"We ought to get some sleep soon," Marick finally stated, breaking their silence, "We're going to need to get an early start to go find samples to get the tests done quickly."

Lance nodded as the pair got up and cleaned themselves in the water basin for the night. Adelade came home, bubbly and happy, expelling all the things she did with her friend. Everyone half-listened to her, not wanting to be rude, but not exactly caring about her playdate. She paid no attention to their automatic responses of "oh yeah?" and "that sounds fun!" She was the first and only one to fall asleep that night, blissfully unaware of what was going on.

Lance kept thinking to himself that it was time to tell Adelade everything. Leaving her in the dark was only going to be a problem. If the Community dissolved or worse, she wouldn't understand what was happening and could compromise their survival. It was something that he couldn't allow, and he was sure his parents would agree with too.

It was time for all hands on deck.

He tried to remember where he heard the line come from. Maybe from Wallais or a book. He rolled over, the thought fleeing his mind.

Lance closed his eyes but didn't fall asleep.

He tossed and turned, listening to the last of the rustling leaves that had yet to fall from the trees. Soon the air would be too silent for him to sleep when Winter would finally settle in. He would get used to the silence and when Spring returned the noise would keep him awake.

It was a vicious cycle.

He tried to relax a bit, thinking of a cool Spring day sitting on a branch and reading his favorite book, *Emir's Education in the Proper Use of Magical Powers*. It was a children's book, but he loved reading over and over Emir's discovery of the importance of nature and life in general. As a child, he would imagine himself as Emir, learning about everything around him, but as he got older he realized that he had nothing in common with the boy in the book but that didn't stop him from reading it over and over again until the pages fell from the binding.

That night sleep would not come, and Lance watched the sun rise through the cracks in the walls and eventually the windows, at which time he forced himself up to get ready when he heard the stirrings of his father across the cabin. As he stood, he stumbled drunkenly from the lack of sleep.

There was a chill in the air that Lance hated. He wanted to stay in the warmth of his bed and forget everything going on around him, but doing that wouldn't solve anything. His problems would still be there when he eventually got up, as would the cold.

He and his father put on their heavier clothing and began walking to the Alabaster Rampart.

"I need to gather some things before we go out. The field test kit is in the storage room in the basement. Once we get that, we can go into the woods."

Lance had his bow and quiver with him, though it was more for protection than hunting. One could never be too sure out in the woods, but he was happy to leave it over his shoulder all day for once.

Despite only going into the woods together to collect samples of toxic soil, Lance was excited to spend some time with his father. The last time they spent time together like this was in Spring earlier that year when his father requested a day off so they could go enjoy the nice weather. They sat against a mossy rock and just took in everything around them, Lance pointing out different animal tracks and noises while Marick told him stories about when he was a child in the Community and the trouble he used to get into with his friends. They laughed like old friends instead of father and son. It was something that he never did with his mother, so time with his father was extra special to him.

They both entered the atrium of the Alabaster Rampart, quietly making their way through the still-silent hallways. The majority of people, both inside and out, were asleep and it was one of the few short times that the Community ever really felt peaceful to Lance. He listened to the soles of his boots rhythmically clap on the tile as they made their way to the grow rooms.

When they finally did arrive, Lance's jaw hit the floor.

All of the planters that once held plants, albeit half dead and scraggly ones, were empty. Not even a grain of dirt was still in them. The plants lay yellow and withered on the floor in a sad pile. Marick's eyes met Lance's but no words escaped his lips. The gravity of the situation was evident. Never in the entirety of his life had Lance seen the grow rooms empty or even heard a story about them being empty. It was as if someone had ransacked the place. The empty pots weren't neatly stacked, they were tossed around the room haphazardly with some in better condition than others which had taken an obvious fall. As they crossed the room, they crunched over pulverized clay pot debris.

"What happened here, Dad?"

"The Elders. They ordered the grow room to be shut down. It wasn't like this earlier. Someone must have had a bit of a meltdown I suppose. Maybe it was Jackie. He was pretty upset when the rooms were closed down and a soil test was ordered. At least not *all* the pots are broken though. I think we can salvage those to get by if we need to."

Lance peeked over his father's shoulder to see some of the porcelain pots stacked neatly against the wall.

"C'mon, we need to go this way," Marick mumbled.

The pair made their way to the back of the grow rooms to a door that Lance had never noticed before. Inside were jars full of seeds on shelves, though some had been turned over and spilled over the floor. There were some empty shelves and a thin layer of dirt over most of the surfaces. Marick moved past these things to a workbench in the back that contained dirt-crusted tools that had seen their fair share of gardening over the decades. The tools bore the scars of makeshift self-repairs with some sporting the tattered remains of duct tape and melted pieces in an effort to stick them back together. It made Lance think of a child destroying their toy, and in a fit of regret, trying to piece it back together. He frowned before looking around the room to see what his father was doing.

Marick pulled a metal box from the bench, opened it and sifted through for a moment, noisily jostling around something inside.

Lance couldn't see what was in the box, but it was obviously what his father was looking for as he tucked it away out of sight and into his rucksack. He then pulled open a drawer that clattered loudly as the glass containers within bounced off each other. He pulled out a half-dozen jars and put them into the bag as well. With a deep breath he turned on his heel, facing Lance and giving him a limp smile.

Lance could tell that his father was hurting, but he didn't say anything. He didn't want to give him a pity pep talk since he was sure it would only make his father feel worse. Instead, he silently hoped that the day together could pick up his mood.

As they walked back through the hallways to the outdoors, the sound of Lance's boots were now accompanied by the hypnotic noise of the clinking jars inside of his father's bag.

"So is there somewhere specific that we need to take the tests from?" Lance asked, desperate to cut through the silence around them.

"Yeah, we take the tests from areas that have an abundance of growth. Generally the thought is that the soil with the most growth has the most nutrient to offer."

"How will you know if it's good to use?"

"I have a few different tests that I run. Some I can do in the field, while some others I will have to do back in the grow room lab later on. I'll be able to tell pretty much right away from the field tests, but doing the chemical tests tells us how much pollution has left the soil since our last test to try and determine a timeline as to when it should be safe to grow plants in it again."

"You're able to tell all of that from those tests?"

"Just about. It's not one hundred percent accurate, but it's as close as we're going to get. We don't have all the technology that the Old World had for these tests to predict the exact time that the pollutants will eek out, but we have enough to tell us if it's safe to use now."

The two men braced themselves as they pushed through the main doors of the Alabaster Rampart into the cold air yet again. He yawned, expelling a large puff of steam into the air. He wiped away his already freezing tears from the corner of his eyes with his sleeve.

"So if the soil is good enough to use, how long until the grow room can start producing food again?"

Marick rubbed the stubble on his tired face before speaking. "Too long. It would be at least two months minimum for plants to be harvested. It could easily take almost three." Marick cast a sideways glance toward Lance. There was a grim expression on his face before the volume of his voice was just above a whisper. "Of course, we have to survive that long without food first."

Lance didn't want to ask anymore questions as he was afraid of bringing down the mood further, so he remained silent as he and his father walked through the village to the forest where he felt the most comfortable. The leaves had not yet completely fallen off the trees, but enough had fallen to allow him to see through small gaps of open space. He wasn't expecting to see any animals in the woods today, but the conversation with his father sparked a twang of anxiety in his gut that made him hopeful that he would so he could bring at least *something* home.

"Do you know of any places where the foliage is most dense?"

He pondered for a moment, thinking of specific places to take his father. It was harder to remember as the browning leaves around him were different from the bright, vibrant shades of green he was so fond of in the Spring and Summer. "I think I know of a few places, but bear with me, it's a little harder to find them now that everything is beginning to go dormant for the Winter."

There was one spot in particular that Lance was thinking of that he knew was full of berries. He would often hide on a tree branch just above a large rock out of sight while he waited for something to come by to munch on the bushes. Coincidentally, it was one of his favorite places in the forest to go and just watch the animals. He would often sit there for hours, his legs going numb, just watching squirrels fight over fallen acorns, birds creating little divots in the dried patches of dirt as they bathed themselves, and watching families of deer move through the area, showing their young what food was safe and what wasn't.

As Lance guided his father through the woods, he mentally noted the difference between the way his parents walked.

He and his mother walked through these woods making practically little to no noise that if they weren't walking next to each other, they would lose sight of one another. But his father on the other hand seemed to know exactly where every branch, patch of gravel and crunching leaf was because he was stepping on them all. If there were any animals in the woods, Marick was surely spooking them away.

"It's nice out here. I can see why you love coming out here. I hate working in that stuffy basement."

"Yeah," Lance agreed, "It's really nice. It's good to get away from all the noise from back home. It's easy to clear your head out here."

"I can imagine. It was strange to walk around home this morning and be able to hear myself think."

"I'm sure the noise from the Community also hasn't been helping with the food situation. I can hear it for at least a quarter mile away. Animals have a better sense of hearing than we do so I'm sure they can hear us from even farther away."

Lance could just see the area he was looking for through the clear patches in the trees.

"Over here," Lance pointed.

The area was bare, but the remnants of the berry bushes were still there along with the fading footprints of some animal that had no doubt indulged itself with the berries. He sighed, thinking of sitting in the tree and reading and how he wouldn't be doing that for quite some time, if at all, depending on if he made it through the Winter.

Marick moved past Lance and knelt down, opening his pack and began to rustle through his items. Lance peered over his shoulder and saw that his father had brandished a jar and shovel. He stabbed the ground, piercing the top of the crust and began to load the little jar up with dirt. Lance was happy that the soil wasn't frozen as it would have made the whole process a lot tougher.

Once Marick packed the dirt into the jar, he pulled out a little plastic glass with some clear water in it. He sprinkled a small clump of dirt in, swirling it around in the jar, turning the water a light brown color.

As the water settled, Lance saw little black particles begin to settle at the bottom. His father pulled out a little paper strip and proceeded to submerge it in the water. They both watched as he pulled the strip out and watched the color change to the same dark red color of rose petals.

Lance didn't need to ask, he knew the color was *not* what they wanted to see.

"Shit," Marick cursed, tossing the paper into the jar of soil before dumping out the little glass. He cleaned it well before he put it along with the soil sample into his bag. He pulled out a scrap piece of paper and scribbled something down before shoving it into his pocket. "So we know where each sample comes from," he noted over his shoulder to Lance.

As the morning slipped into afternoon, they stopped at three other spots and found the same little red strip coming out of the water each time. It was at the sixth and final jar that Marick just sat down on the ground, shoulders slumped and looked up at his son like a child that just broken his favorite toy.

Lance took his bow and quiver from off his shoulders and gently placed them on the ground before taking a seat next to his father in the dirt. He propped his right arm on his bent knee and looked out over the woods. Despite Winter being ready to set in, he could still hear chirping birds in the distance that would be staying put to brave the cold. He took a deep breath and let it loose, easing a tension in his chest that he hadn't noticed before.

"We're proud of you, your mother and me. You know that right? I don't think we say it enough," his father blurted out.

Lance looked at his father and smiled before returning his gaze to the woods.

"I feel like *you're* proud, but I don't know about Mom. She's been pretty irritated with me lately, but not without a good reason."

Marick dismissed Lance's comment with a scoff and a wave of his hand.

"Your mother is proud, believe me, she is. I see it on her face every time you bring back food. Even when you don't, I still see it in her eyes. She's just worried about the Community. Every time food isn't brought back home it makes her nervous for the future. She's proud of the man you've become just like I am. She just has a bad way of showing it. Besides, you and I both know that she would've started a fight in the canteen if it was you that was hit with that soup."

Lance smiled and said, "I had great parents to bring me up. I'm glad I have you guys."

"We're glad to have *you*. Imagine if we got stuck with Jasper?"

They both laughed, which felt great to do, despite their circumstance.

Marick glanced down at the bag with a frown. He went to speak but Lance put up a hand and stopped him.

"I know, Dad. We'll be okay."

"With you and your mother, we won't just survive, we'll thrive. We'll figure out something," he said with a smile.

The pair just sat for a moment together, not speaking, not thinking of going back to the Community, or what they were going to eat tonight for supper. They were thinking about how nice of a day it was, and how not many of these were left before the snow would roll in and keep them shut in their cabin for months shivering from the cold seeping through the cracks of their walls.

That is until a thought popped into Lance's head.

"We need to tell Addie what's going on in the Community," Lance blurted, turning his gaze to his father.

Marick looked stunned, his mouth agape. "W-well, how do you propose we do that?"

"We need to just tell her. I get that we want her to be a kid for as long as possible, but that is only going to make things worse for her when the shit really hits the fan. She won't be ready and it would be worse than telling her it is going to happen now."

Marick nodded. "I've been thinking the same thing to be honest with you. I've been trying to find a way to bring it up to your mother, but I didn't want to put more on her plate. Plus, I didn't really want to start an argument with her. You know how she is when she has her mind set on something."

Lance clucked his tongue. His mother was too set in her ways for them to convince her otherwise, though it couldn't hurt to at least try.

"Let me try and do it. Worst case scenario, I just pull Adelade away for a bit and tell her myself."

"No, let's do it together. Sneaking around is just going to cause more problems. I'm sure she'll be on board with us after we explain things," Marick reasoned.

Lance gave his father a confident smile. Despite the bad results they got from the soil test, today was a good day. Spending time with his Dad was always good no matter what they were doing.

"We should be getting back. I still have to run the chemical tests," Marick announced, standing up and gathering his things.

Lance followed suit and the pair trudged back to the Community. They heard the hustle and bustle from within the village before they saw it. Lance raised his eyebrows at his father as if to say, "Told you".

Marick shook his head and smiled.

They entered the compound and separated at the front doors to the Rampart.

"Remember, tonight we both talk to her," Marick reminded, "Don't do it without me. You have your mother's attitude and I know you will unless I say something."

Lance scoffed, "Go play with your dirt. I'll see you later."

They laughed, embraced, and went their separate ways.

Lance beamed as he waded through the crowd of people back to his cabin. He had all but forgotten the bad results of the PH test today and had instead thought of his father's words in the forest. His parents were proud and that was all he could ask for.

"Hey, Mom," he greeted as he walked into the cabin. He kicked off his boots, dropped his gear and began bathing in the wash basin.

"How did the soil test go?"

Lance dried his face on a rag, his smile fading.

"As expected. The soil around here isn't any good. Dad is going to run some tests back at the lab in the grow room, but there's no way we're going to be growing out there anytime soon."

Her shoulders slumped. "Shit."

"We'll figure something out. Don't worry," he said, trying to instil some confidence in his mother as he had done with his father earlier.

She gave him a look. "What's got you in such a good mood?"

"I had a good time with Dad today. I'm trying to focus on that."

She sat down at the table and buried her face in her hands, her long hair spilling over and hiding her face.

"What did you and Adelade do today?" Lance asked, trying to change the subject before his mother ruined his mood.

"I watched her draw more dogs. Then she wanted to go to a friend's house."

As if on cue before Lance could ask which friend, the door burst open and Adelade came bolting in. "Lance," she screamed as she leapt into his lap and squeezed the air from him.

"Hi, Addie," he croaked, trying to return the hug with an even enthusiasm.

"Guess where I was?"

"I don't know, where were you?" he asked with exaggerated curiosity.

"I went to Steven's house today. Do you know that he gets to draw on his walls? Mom, can I draw on the walls?"

Lance and Shushannah exchanged glances.

"No way," they said in unison.

5

She hated the smell of the wood inside of the cabin. It was crafted from freshly cut pine trees but the smell only made her think of her and her family's expulsion from the Alabaster Rampart. She had been sitting in the corner of the little cabin with her arms crossed and a scowl cemented her on face, and no amount of coaxing from her parents could remove it.

"Shushannah," her father, Gabriel snapped, "Enough is enough young lady! Sitting here and pouting will not change our situation. If anything, you're making things worse for all of us! You think that I like living out here? Do you think that I like the fact that we were removed from our home where we had running water and electricity to *this* shithole?! Well if you think I do, you're dead wrong! So instead of sitting in the corner and blaming your mother and me, make yourself scarce and go practice your archery like you *should* be doing."

She returned her father's command with a stern glare, which he mimicked without uttering another syllable.

Without taking her eyes off of her father, she stomped across the house, snatched up her bow and quiver, and left for the woods to find a tree to take out her frustrations on. There was no way that she would be winning that argument with him. Hell, she *never* won an argument with him. He was always pushing and pushing her. She didn't dare utter the words, but on the inside she was beginning to resent him. She was never allowed out with friends from her class, was never allowed toys or crayons like the other children, and she was always out in the woods practicing her archery until the tips of her fingers were about to split open.

Even though she was only eight years old, she was a much better shot than her old man who had been hunting well before she was born. She hated the monotony of practicing over and over again, but as long as she stayed sharp, she could join her father in the woods one day to hunt. When she eventually did, she felt proud of herself as she nearly tripled what her father found. Back then, animals were everywhere you looked, but it was different now.

The population had grown quite a bit larger since she was born, to at least two hundred people in total, making the Alabaster Rampart extremely cramped inside. With people fighting amongst each other for personal space, the Elders selected members of the Community that had children within the last decade and told them they had to construct their own living quarters on the outer grounds. Shushannah didn't want to move outside from the comfort she had been grown up with. She felt like they were all being punished for something when they didn't do anything wrong. She had thrown a tantrum that only was rewarded by a quick slap on her rear by her father to make her to snap out of it.

Tightly clutching her bow and quiver, she retreated to the woods where she began to count to herself how many times she hit the tree in the center of the bark with an arrow. Her father would demand a count from her when she returned, and if he didn't like the number, he would drag her back out and stand with her until the arrows had pierced through the bark of the tree. By that time, her arms would be so tired, it would require all of her effort just to nock an arrow.

She had been shooting at an oak tree for about a half an hour when the sound of heavy footsteps came up behind her. Gabriel appeared through the foliage with a grim expression. She ignored him and continued shooting at the tree as she had been trained to do the last two years she had been practicing.

After her last arrow found a home in the heavily chewed up bark of the tree, she approached it without looking at her father. She yanked the arrows from their spots, slipping them into her quiver and turned on her heel.

"I see places that you missed your mark," he pointed out. He stepped over to the tree and pointed to the dents near the edge of the tree's rounded trunk where an arrow just narrowly struck. He was frowning at her.

"Again," he commanded, "But this time with a new tree and I don't want to see any stray marks."

She fired arrows for another hour until her arms hurt so bad that she couldn't raise them to brush a loose strand of hair from her face.

"Enough," Gabriel stated flatly.

Without another word, he turned and trudged back to the Community.

She found her own way back home, being sure to walk extra slow so that she wouldn't catch up to her father. She found a spot to sit for a while in the center of what would be the new village and watched as some of the newer families slowly made progress on putting together their homes. Some children ran around giggling loudly while playing some game that Shushannah was not familiar with, nor would she ever be. She was not allowed. Although it was her father that had ordered her to stay away from the other children, she was beginning to develop a distaste for the other children around her, but more importantly, had fully developed a distaste for her father who caused her to feel this way, finally realizing just how much he had cheated her out of.

Marick didn't return home until later that night. He pushed open the door and lumbered into the house with his shoulders slumped and dark circles under his eyes illuminated by the moonlight. He shuffled across the floorboards without uttering a single word. Lance followed him with his eyes from his recently fluffed pile of blankets through the holes in his drawn curtains.

His father stopped over the washbasin, supporting himself over the bowl with both hands for a moment. He didn't move or make a noise. Lance could just make out through the darkness rhythmic moving shoulders, up and down, up and down, as he pulled air into his lungs. Finally, he splashed his hands into the water and cleaned his face. He then shuffled over to the bed he shared with Shushannah and collapsed with no further movement.

Lance rolled over onto his side, facing the wall, and chewed his bottom lip. There were going to be some changes taking place for sure.

Lance hadn't realized that he fell asleep until he felt his mother's toe sharply nudging him awake by prodding him in the small of his back. He rubbed the agitated spot where her toenail poked him. "Your father says we need to talk," she grumbled. She was obviously still trying to wake up as her hair was disheveled and her eyes were only half open.

He stretched, listening to the bones of his spine crackle while a groan escaped his lips. He stood, rubbing the sleep from his eyes and dragged himself over to the table where his mother and father sat.

"The samples were no good," Lance stated flatly as he sat down at the table, already knowing from his father's actions last night.

Marick shook his head, his eyes were locked in place, looking down at the surface of the gnarled table. He looked like he hadn't slept a wink.

"They were terrible, but we already knew that was going to happen. What we all need to speak about right now is Adelade." Lance's eyes darted over to his mother, reading her bewildered face.

He then looked around for Adelade to see if she was within earshot and saw her snoozing away in her bundle of blankets, blissfully unaware as always.

"What do you mean? Why do we need to talk about her?" Shushannah asked.

"Lance and I had a talk yesterday while out in the woods and I think if you hear the points too, that you'll agree with us. Adelade needs to know what is going on with the food situation and the Community as a whole. It's only a matter of time before she finds out and it could be problematic unless we clarify it now with her on our own terms before things get too bad."

Lance held his breath without breaking his stare at his mother expecting her to explode with rage at being left out of the conversation. She was thinking with her eyes looking from Lance to Marick. "Okay," she finally said, allowing Lance to release his breath.

"Good," Marick said, "I was worried we would have to convince you. You know how you can be when you get your mind set on something."

Shushannah scoffed but she wasn't visibly upset. "No," she began, "I honestly had been thinking about it myself these past few weeks. You are both right, if we don't explain things now, it will only cause problems in the future. Let's let her sleep for a little bit longer, but we should do this sooner rather than later. Let's talk to her this morning about it. There's no better time like the present I suppose."

Both Lance and Marick nodded in agreement. This was something that needed to be taken care of now.

"Good," she continued, "Now, since the tests were shitty, are the Elders aware of this?"

"They are. When I presented them with the results last night before coming home they said that they would be calling a Community meeting today to announce the results to everyone and to see if anyone has any possible solutions they want to contribute."

"Did they say what time?"

Marick should his head. "No, but I imagine it will be earlier in the day, perhaps this afternoon. They probably want to jump in front of this thing before it gets too far out of hand."

Shushannah tugged at her bottom lip with her tooth before

speaking. "Alright," she announced and walked over to Adelade and gently shook her awake. "Hey, wake up sleepyhead," she cooed, "There's something we need to talk to you about, okay? It's important." There was a tenderness in her voice that Lance tried to ignore as a pang of jealousy quickly shot through him.

He directed his attention to the frost-covered window as Adelade struggled to get out of bed with Shushannah's help.

Adelade came over to the table and sat on her legs in a chair, her eyes lolling in her head as she fought to keep them open. Her hair was in need of brushing and Lance had to stifle a laugh while looking at her bedraggled appearance.

"Honey, there's something really important that we need to talk to you about," Marick started softly, somewhat catching her attention.

"What is it?" she groaned, wiping her eyes again with her hands that were balled into tight little fists. Watching her try to wake up made Lance feel even more tired. He hid a large yawn behind the back of his left hand and blinked away the mistiness that had gathered in his eyes.

"Lately there have been some bad things happening in the Community. We haven't been completely honest with you about it, but we will be now and moving forward, okay?. I'm sure that by now you may have noticed some strange things going on lately in the Community."

Adelade let out a sigh. "No, I already know."

"You do?" Shushannah blurted in disbelief, "How?"

"Mommy, kids in school talk. I hear you, Daddy, and Lance talk, I hear the people around here talk, and I hear the Elders talk. I'm not deaf and you guys always do it in front of me."

Everyone was silent while Adelade looked at each one of them without emotion. Lance sat back in his chair with his arms folded over his chest. He laughed to himself, realizing how stupid he felt, underestimating his little sister and reflecting back to his own childhood days of sneaking around and listening to conversations he shouldn't.

"What's so funny over there?" Shushannah asked with genuine concern.

"I should have known that she wasn't completely in the dark. Kids listen more than we think, Mom. I was a kid once too, and not that long ago. I was nosey as hell. I bet you and Dad were too."

Marick began to laugh now too. Shushannah was still visibly confused.

"Mom, did you not listen in on your parents or neighbors talk as a kid? Did you not want to listen to what the adults were talking about when they sent you to bed or sent you away to talk about 'grown-up stuff'?"

"I don't remember to be completely honest. I don't think about my childhood that often," she said quietly, her eyes looking passed Lance and at wall.

Lance stared at the solemn look that had formed on his mother's face. He had never seen her make that face before. It was strange to see his mother without a stern look. Normally, she was the one holding everyone together like glue, pulling herself up by her bootstraps first and then forcing the others to. She sat like that for a moment before she caught him looking at her, at which time she blinked a couple times and reset her face to her usual, much more familiar, scowl.

She did not meet his eyeline again though Lance did not go searching to make her feel more uncomfortable than she already was.

"So, honey," Marick started, taking over for Shushannah and redirecting the conversation back to the matter at hand, "Do you understand how serious things are right now? Do you know that we need to be careful?"

"Of the Founders," she answered, though it was in the form of a question more so than a confident reply.

"Well, yes, but more importantly we need to be careful with our food. You see, Daddy can't grow any more food right now, and there aren't many animals out in the woods to hunt, so we may have to only eat once a day, or maybe less, for a little while. Do you understand?"

Lance looked at his sister's little face that had contorted itself into a grimace. If her brain were a machine, gears would be turning and smoke would pour from her ears while she processed the information, trying to make sense of it. Her mouth opened and closed again. He could tell she didn't want to disappoint Marick with a wrong answer.

He was about to interrupt her when she finally said, "I understand. You all have already been doing that right? I remember there were some times when we all sat to eat that one of you wouldn't be eating." She paused for a moment, a sudden realization coming to her. "Were all of you giving me your meals?"

Nobody wanted to say anything. They looked at each other, wondering how to best answer her question.

"Yeah, we have," Lance answered, deciding the direct route was best at this point.

Adelade cast her face down to her lap.

"Don't feel bad. We did it for you and we would all do it again," Lance said with pride, looking to his parents to agree with him.

"Yes, listen to your brother," Shushannah spoke up, "We would do it a hundred times and more for you."

Adelade had tears in her eyes as she looked up and around the table at her family members. She let out either a happy gasp or a slight sob, but she was smiling nonetheless. Shushannah was the first to stand and wrap her arms tightly around the child. Both Lance and Marick followed Shushannah's lead and formed one big family hug and they stayed like that for a few minutes. They eventually stepped away from Adelade who was no longer crying but was still beaming up at them all.

They didn't speak any further on the subject, feeling relieved to have it done and over with as it was one less thing to worry about.

Eventually, Lance had decided to go and visit Wallais for a bit since he and his mother wouldn't be going out hunting until the following day. He hadn't seen his friend for quite some time, and he was sure that Wallais could use a friend to get his mind off things just as Lance needed.

He walked through the village towards the Alabaster Rampart, silently observing the other Outsiders go about their business. Most people were scurrying around, hurrying this way and that with dread and uncertainty cemented to their weary faces. Word was surely getting around by now about the grow rooms being shut down. Despite this, it was business as usual in the village as people were busy making any needed repairs to houses to prepare for the oncoming winter months, the blacksmith was hard at work making what looked like kitchen utensils from broken hunks of metal the Founders threw out, and there were kids running around playing some sort of game that only made sense if you were in their world with them to see what their imaginations had created. He thought of his own childhood, dredging up the memories from when he would be dragged through the village by his mother to the woods where she would teach him how to hunt. He remembered wanting to be playing with the other children; running, screaming, laughing; having fun—not killing animals.

He still found himself wishing that he could lock himself away somewhere and just act like a kid again, even if it were only for a little bit. He felt like he was starved of something important.

For the final days of Autumn, it was a beautiful day outside. The sun was shining brightly, the sky was empty of clouds and on the surface it appeared as if there was nothing wrong in the world. Even the temperature was warmer than normal.

He walked into the atrium of the Alabaster Rampart and his mind flashed back to the first day he ever met Wallais which was right in that very room.

It was his first day of school and his father was bringing him in before his shift in the grow rooms. He hadn't slept a wink the night before and was nervous about his first day. He was used to wasting away his days playing in the cabin while he waited for his family to come home from work and he didn't like the idea of going to school with a bunch of kids he didn't know. He was watched every day by an elderly woman that lived in the village. He couldn't remember her face clearly, though he knew her only by "Ethel". She passed away shortly after he started school when a deadly stomach virus made its way through the Community.

His father had tried his best to calm him down that morning but it wasn't going so well. He was tugging on his father's arm, digging the heels of his shoes into the tile to try and turn back. He was willing to do anything to get out of going to school, even throwing a temper tantrum. Nothing was beneath him if it would get him what he wanted.

Beatrice was standing with a welcoming smile at the front entrance of the Rampart to greet the new children from the village so she could show them the way to the classroom. Wallais was standing beside her, chewing on his thumb amongst a group of children that were all starting school that day too. Marick brought Lance over, though it was more of a forceful push instead of guiding as he was tired of fighting with Lance to get him to school.

"It appears someone is a bit nervous to start school," Beatrice cooed down to him. She was smiling as she watched Marick push him across the hallway to the little group, and she continued to do so as he shifted on his little feet nervously.

"Why don't you meet my son, Wallais? I think you two would be great friends." She winked at Marick as she gently took Lance under her right arm. He looked back at his father who waved with a smile before marching off to work. Lance fought to keep tears back as he watched his father leave him. He felt deserted, cheated, wronged.

Just before they reached the other children, she bent down on one knee and whispered into Lance's ear, "He's nervous too, but don't worry, there's nothing to be scared of. Sometimes having a friend through a tough time makes things easier."

Lance remembered those words for the entirety of his life. He felt better knowing that he wasn't the only one nervous about facing the challenges of the world. It was when he first met Wallais that he knew everything would be alright. They laughed together the entire first day of school and were basically inseparable from that moment on. He smiled to himself as the memory faded away and returned to the back of his mind where he would be sure to recall it again in the future as he liked to do from time to time when he needed a pick-me-up.

His body automatically knew the path to get to Wallais's home as he had walked there himself more times than he could count.

He opened the door without knocking and was immediately slapped on the back, sending him stumbling forward. "Lance," Ogden boomed, "How are you?"

Lance rubbed his shoulder and gave Ogden a smile. "I'm doing alright. Is Wallais around?"

Ogden smiled a toothy smile as per usual. "He's in his room. He'll be glad to see you. He's been pretty down in the dumps since the results of the soil testing came back. He could really use a friend."

"That's what I'm here for. I'll have him back to his old self in no time."

"Good," Ogden said before slapping Lance one last time with a hearty chuckle.

Lance retreated back to Wallais's room rubbing his sore, and probably already bruising, shoulder. He reminded himself that he would need to avoid Ogden for a bit, otherwise it would never heal.

He found Wallais's door slightly open, with Wallais sprawled out on his stomach on his bed reading a book. He hadn't noticed Lance enter the room yet, so as if he were tracking prey, Lance crouched and stalked over to his friend, careful not to make a noise, before yelling, "Hi, Wallais," at the top of his lungs, causing Wallais to flail about, flinging his book across the room. Lance had just enough time to move his head to the right to avoid the book hitting him square in the face. Wallais put his hand to his chest and took a few breaths before playfully punching Lance in the arm.

"Asshole," he breathed once he was able to catch his breath.

"Miss me?" Lance gave him a toothy smile.

"Fuck, no you dick."

The boys gave their usual greeting embrace before settling down on the floor.

"So how's it going?" Lance asked immediately, a more serious tone in his voice.

Wallais shrugged. "It could be better. I'm sure you heard about the soil test results and the grow room being shut down. I don't know what we're going to do."

Lance sighed through his nose, the same thought bugging his mind as well. "I know. There haven't been any animals in the woods to bring back, but I think this is only temporary."

Lance was trying to find the confidence in his voice to try and bring his friend's mood up, but it came out sounding forced.

"What makes you say that?"

Lance shrugged. "I just do. Something deep inside is telling me that things are going to work out. Trust me," then a thought came to him, "Besides, between you and me, I was thinking about risking going beyond the Edge."

Wallais's eyes bulged from his skull the same way they had when they were kids and he looked as if Lance had just punted a baby across the village square. He shot up from the bed and closed his door. He turned on his heel and whispered, though it came out more like a hoarse hissing noise, "Are you crazy? You know there isn't anything past the Edge! That would be suicide to go out there!"

Lance met Wallais's eyeline with a calm, confident gaze.

"I don't think it's dangerous out there. There's too many unanswered questions. Where do you think all the animals come from? Where do you think that they disappear to? What about the other Communities that started before ours when the Old World bit the dust? I can't fully believe that there isn't anything out there. Animals don't just appear out of thin air. If they did, we wouldn't be on the verge of starving to death."

Wallais seemed to have calmed down quite a bit after hearing Lance's reasoning. He pondered the thought carefully, gnawing on the inside of his cheek.

"Alright, you have a point," he finally admitted, "But how do you plan on going out there?"

"I'll figure it out. Honestly, I haven't put much thought into *how* I would get out there, but more along the lines that we *needed* to get out there. I still need to bring it up to my Mom, and she's probably not going to like the idea very much. Worst case scenario, I just sneak out there myself one day and prove that it's safe."

"What if you find out that it isn't what you think though? What if something happens to you and nobody knows where you are?"

"That's why I'll tell you the day before I decide to go out there. If I don't come back, tell someone, and then we know not to go out there. I'm not crazy, Wallais, I wouldn't be going out there if there was another way. We're all likely to die from starvation anyway. I would rather die beyond the Edge trying to save my family and yours than to sit around and watch you all starve to death."

Wallais met Lance's eyes and saw the confidence behind them. That was all it took for him to be on board with the idea. When they were kids, Lance would give him the same look if he had any doubts, whether that be sneaking out to play in the woods or sneaking into the kitchens to steal scraps of food. Each time Lance gave Wallais that look they always made it back safe and sound. "Then I'm with you," Wallais said.

"I know you are. You always are." Lance smiled at his friend—no, his brother. They bumped fists before Lance stood up.

"I have to head back. I should talk to my Mom about this tonight—put the bug in her ear about it. Let's keep this between us for now, alright? I'll let you know when it's safe to tell the others about it. I don't want everyone to panic just yet."

"You got it. See you soon?"

"For sure. I'll swing by again soon."

Lance managed to slip out of Wallais's home without getting another beating from Ogden much to his relief. He had managed to get halfway down the hallway towards the stairs when a strong hand grabbed him, spinning him around and pushing him against the wall. It was Seamus and he did *not* look happy.

"Please tell me I didn't hear you correctly in there," he whispered, his eyes darting around to be sure that there were no eavesdroppers around to listen in on their conversation.

Lance clenched his jaw and moved in closer to Seamus to keep their volume level down. "You did. Seamus, there is no more food. There are no grow rooms, there's nothing out in the woods. I *have* to do this, otherwise we're all as good as dead."

Seamus breathed heavily through his nose and shook his head in irritation. "You're like a brother to me, Lance. I know you and I don't have the same relationship that you have with Wallais, but I've known you long enough to consider you a family member and I can't in good conscience let you go past the Edge."

"Then what do you propose I do? Would you rather we all starve? Because unless you have an answer to this Community's problem, there is no other choice." Lance's voice was rising as his rage and panic piled onto each other. Seamus could jeopardize the entire plan.

"I'd rather we think about this rationally."

"I *am*."

Lance could feel his anger simmering, waiting to explode.

"Are you? Are you really? Or are you thinking out of fear?"

It was Lance's turn to shake his head.

"I'm thinking like someone that wants to survive. Would you rather sit here and wait to die, or would you rather find a solution to our problem? If we don't do anything we are as good as dead anyways. How long can we survive on boiled water? Do you propose we eat our clothes? They're almost in worse shape than we are. What do you think is going to get us out of this shit? Action is the only thing that will save us now, not sitting around."

A sudden clap of approval jolted the men from their conversation.

They turned to see the Elders standing before them. Elder Sampson was clapping with a smile on his face. "Well said, Lance. You are indeed correct that action needs to be taken at this time. I ask that both of you report back to your families. We are calling a formal town meeting to discuss our current situation. Lance, after the meeting, we would like to speak with both yourself and your mother."

Lance swallowed a lump in his throat. He didn't speak and only shakily nodded his head in agreement.

With a quick glance to an equally nervous Seamus he departed from the Alabaster Rampart and rushed home, keeping his head down with his mind racing about what the Elders were going to say at the meeting and then later to himself and his mother. He moved quickly, so quick in fact, that he didn't realize he was in a direct path into Jasper. The two roughly bumped into each other, effectively bring Lance back to the real world.

"Watch where you're going asshole," Jasper spat.

"Fuck you, *you* watch where you're going," Lance retorted automatically.

He shoved passed Jasper, and quickly continued on his path, not in the headspace to deal with Jasper. Now was not the time. He heard Jasper shout something at him, but he didn't hear it or care to hear it. It wouldn't be anything he hadn't heard before, and to be honest, Jasper was the least of his concerns right now.

Lance came into his cabin to find his father sitting on the floor with Adelade drawing pictures. They both looked up at him smiling. Shushannah was nowhere to be found in their little house. Her hunting gear was missing, which answered his question.

"The Elders are calling a meeting," he blurted. Marick's smile fell and he began to gather the coloring supplies. Adelade noticed the serious look on her father and brother's face and understood immediately that the time for fun would have to wait. She helped Marick put things away hastily, looking concerned.

They were silent as they left their home and walked to the meeting area at the landing of the Alabaster Rampart. Some people were already there waiting. Over the course of the next ten minutes or so, families trickled in from the village and faces appeared in the windows as both Founders and Outsiders received word that the meeting would be starting shortly. Lance never really paid attention to their numbers before, but most likely due to the food crisis, today he noticed just how many people there were.

From where he stood, he could see at least a hundred people at minimum standing outside, and at least another sixty faces in the panes of glass. He knew that there were more people that he could not see standing behind those in the windows. Their numbers had grown exponentially over the years as child after child was born.

He scanned the crowd, looking to see if his mother was returning. He stopped a moment later thinking better of it as she could be out all afternoon and well into the night if it meant getting even just a scrap of meat.

After what felt like an eternity, the Elders finally stepped out onto their platform dressed in their usual garb, dark robes made of the last of the fabrics from the Old World, though due to the cold weather, they had adorned their fur-lined robes. Elder Sampson was in the lead as per their usual custom. Elder Maxwell was on Sampson's right side, crossing his arms, but not sporting his usual scowl and instead appeared to almost have a grin on his face. Elder Borris was standing idly on Sampson's other side scanning the crowd, undoubtedly taking in their large numbers just as Lance was moments before. A dull murmur had been vibrating through the air that Lance hadn't noticed until Elder Sampson raised his hand to hush the crowd as he had done so many times before. Silence fell after rushed shushes from various members of the Community, all wishing to hear Sampson speak. He smiled over the crowd, panning from left to right and then back to facing forward before speaking.

"Good afternoon," he began, "I would like to begin like always by welcoming you all here today," he paused and looked over the crowd again before continuing, "We have had a very rough year this year—the roughest by far—and yet here we all stand. I want to tell you all how proud I am of you, and I wish to have us give thanks to those who worked day and night to supply us with food to get us to the point we are today."

An unenthusiastic clapping broke out through the crowd.

"As you all know, food has been scarce as of late, and due to the incoming cold weather, most hunted game will be hiding away from the cold, which means they will be hiding from *us*. Our food supply has run dangerously low—the lowest that it has ever been. A short while ago, we came to the understanding that the soil used in the grow rooms was void of all nutrients and would not sustain plant life. We sent one of our growers to the forest to conduct a test of various spots that could be suitable for soil harvesting to begin preparations for a new round of growing, and a goal time to get by until for the next harvest."

Elder Sampson's face grew dark before the next words came out of his mouth that crushed the remaining glimmer of hope that the people of Community: 1049 had left.

"The soil test results that we received told us that the soil in the woods is highly contaminated with pollutants still, and any food grown from it will surely kill us. As there is no usable soil for growing our much needed crops, we have at this time ceased all work in the grow rooms and will need to begin rationing out the remainder of our food."

Hushed whispers hung in the air as the crowds anxiety levels grew. Despite Sampson raising a hand to quiet the dull roar, it had no effect. Instead of lowering his hand, he kept it raised until finally someone noticed and began the shushing once again.

"Thank you," he stated, "As we speak, we are looking to come up with possible solutions to our dilemma. Should these not work, we will resort to a more dire plan that the council has discussed in length. We ask that anyone with possible ideas please do not hesitate to bring them up. Make no mistake, we are in dire times, but I assure you all, we will get through this!"

He stopped talking for a moment, looking over the crowd. Lance was sure he expected applause, but naturally only silence hung in the air.

"I would like to request the presence of all hunters in our chambers within the next half an hour. At this point we have finished our meeting. Once we have completed our discussion with the hunters, we will begin taking in community members to discuss any possible solutions you may have. Thank you."

Elder Sampson turned and retreated to the interior of the Alabaster Rampart with Elder Maxwell and Elder Borris in tow. Lance stood still for a moment, knowing that things were about to get a lot worse for the Community.

"Before I go, I need to tell you something," Lance said to Marick in a low voice, being sure to avoid anyone from hearing, "The Elders overheard me speaking with Seamus before the meeting was called. I had been talking with Wallais about going past the Edge and he overheard. I think the Elders heard me talking about it with Seamus and they may be sending us out there."

Marick was mortified. "Why would you even think to do such a thing?! The Elders have been harping for years about the pollution levels out there! It would be suicide! What if things change? What if you go past the Edge and die for nothing? I can't lost you, Lance. I won't, and I damn well know that your mother won't let you either."

"Dad, keep your voice down," Lance hissed, "I was thinking that going past the Edge could save the Community. Who's to say that things are worse beyond the Edge? Nobody has ever gone to *look*! What if there's better hunting grounds or safe soil? What if we're the only bad spot left on the planet and we find a safe place to live? I don't want to starve to death wondering what's out there when I could go and see for myself."

Marick made the same face that Seamus did earlier, but instead of disagreeing with his son, he said, "Okay. If this is what you truly believe, I trust you. I hear you. Maybe this is for the best. You go to the Elder's chambers and I'll fill your mother in when she gets back should she come home before you do."

"Thanks, Dad."

"You really are your mother's son, Lance. I know she would be proud of you to hear those words coming out of your mouth."

Lance felt his face grow warm as his cheeks flushed with embarrassment at the compliment. He was sure his mother would be contesting everything he just said, but he let it go. He did after all need to go to the Chamber of the Elders to undoubtedly talk about the Edge. "I'll be home as soon as I can to tell you guys what the plan is."

His father nodded and Lance gave Adelade a tight hug before trotting off towards the massive structure looming over him. He thought to himself just before opening the large double doors to the Alabaster Rampart that he had been in the Chamber of the Elders more times in the last month than he had been his entire life. He hoped that his visit would have a more positive outcome than the others.

6

Lance sat in between Ogden and Seamus while trying to avoid making eye-contact with Jasper who was over to his left and shooting a dagger-filled stare in his direction. He folded his arms across his chest and tried to focus on the Elders who were, per usual, sitting in sustained silence and staring at the group of hunters seated in front of them. Lance contemplated to himself if this was a power thing or if they were simply just trying to determine what they should say. Either way, Lance couldn't stand it and he wished that they would stop.

After what felt like an eternity, he dropped his arms and shifted uncomfortably in his chair, trying to spark some feeling in his numbing ass.

This felt like more torture than having to do sanitation duty. This would have been a better punishment for his fight with Timothy instead of making him clean up bathrooms. That, or if they forced him to listen to Jasper's incessant bragging about his successful hunting trips that he seemed to *always* have even though there hadn't been any meat in the perpetual stew until Lance brought back that dead deer.

After finally having enough, his mother's attitude once again reared its head and he loudly cleared his throat. Ogden's elbow bumped him sharply in the side. If the Elders noticed this, they didn't react much, though all three sets of eyes were now looking at Lance's grumpy face.

"You are undoubtedly all aware of the dire straits the forest's animal populace is in," Sampson began without breaking eye contact with Lance. There was an emotionless tone to his voice as he spoke. "In the last two weeks, nobody in this room has been able to bring back so much as a rabbit for the Community to eat. We are at a very troubling time, the toughest that the Community has ever seen since it was first established. Over the decades, we have seen our fair share of issues, from sickness to droughts, but this is something that threatens the very existence of the Community as we cannot put temporary measures in place to counter this problem as we have done in the past."

Sampson paused and looked over each face seated in front of him to let his words sink in. Lance had to keep from rolling his eyes at the theatrics.

"Over the course of our time here running Community: 1049, we have spoken outwardly regarding the Edge. As we are the last surviving Community left on the planet, we are aware that there are dangers that await us beyond the borders of our woods. You have all heard us before, warning those of you brave enough to enter the forest, the area past the Edge is home to the more polluted parts of the planet. From what past communications have told us, the air in some areas is toxic to breathe, let alone to sustain any other forms of life. However, with that being said, we have discussed amongst the three of us and came to the decision that we need to send someone past the Edge in order to be *sure* that we are exhausting all of our options."

Audible gasps could be heard in the room with the exception of Lance and Seamus, who were already aware of this development from their interaction only a few hours ago. He could feel Seamus's eyes looking at him though he actively avoided his stare by staying focused on the Elders, setting his jaw and waiting for the rest of Sampson's speech.

"We understand the shock this gives you all given how adamantly we stated the danger of traveling beyond the border of our woods.

Keeping this information in mind, only two of you will be chosen to go beyond the forest's edge and will report back to determine if and what danger is out there and if it is worth risking to feed our people. We have already made the decision as to who will go as it is important that we send able-bodied hunters out with the highest chance of returning home."

The room was silent as Elder Sampson's words hung in the air like a dense, summer morning fog. Lance took stock of the people in the room with him. Sitting with Jasper was another Founder named Derrik who was not hiding his nervousness well as he chewed his lip and vigorously bounced his legs. On either side of Lance sat Ogden and Seamus who were both anxious as well, though they hid it much better than Derrik, but they were both fidgeting in their seats. Next to Seamus was another pair of hunters, Craig and Brandon, a couple of older Founders that Lance didn't interact with. He said "Hi" to them once and the greeting was never returned. It didn't bother him too much, as they kept out of each other's way, and he *really* didn't need another Jasper hanging around.

To Lance, no one in the room had anything to be nervous about because he knew for a fact that they wouldn't be chosen. Lance knew that since he and his mother were the only two Outsiders among the hunters that meant they were "able-bodied"—or in a more obvious meaning: expendable. So when the next words came out of Sampson's mouth, Lance didn't even so much as blink.

"We believe Shushannah and Lance are the best choice for this assignment as they have demonstrated time and time again that they possess the necessary skills that one would need in order to return from a journey such as this. However, I please ask that the rest of you don't take their compliment personally as you are all great hunters and it was no easy decision to make."

Ogden and Seamus both shifted uncomfortably in their seats while Jasper cast a smug glance over to Lance. Of course he wouldn't have been chosen, not with his father being one of the Elders. Even if he was the only hunter the Community had he wouldn't have been sent out because some other poor fool would have been sent in out in his place. Lance ignored Jasper, keeping his seething temper under control. He nodded confidently to the Elders, showing everyone in the room that he was not deterred in the slightest about being chosen to undergo this task.

"We thank you for being so cooperative with us on this matter, Lance," Sampson thanked him with a smile, though it was more for appearances rather than for truly being grateful as Lance and Shushannah didn't *really* have a choice in the matter.

"You are all free to go now. Lance, please fill your mother in regarding our decision and we will send Peter, our newest runner, to you tomorrow when we have a plan in place for you and your mother. Thank you all again for coming to us at such short notice."

Everyone stood from the uncomfortable chairs and exited the room in single-file fashion. Lance did so with a limp as pins and needles ran up and down his right leg as feeling slowly returned to his ass. He grumbled to himself as he rubbed his thigh.

"Good thing I wasn't picked," Jasper emphasized with obvious sarcasm once the door to the Elders' Chambers closed, "I wouldn't know what to do if I was. I'm happy that the two *able-bodied* members of our group have the situation under control!"

Ogden hurriedly pushed Lance along, towards their apartment thinking that a fight would erupt. Lance brushed his hand away gently with a grin. He was well aware of what Jasper was attempting to do, but it fell on deaf ears, he had control over his rage and refused to let Jasper get to him. Jasper disappeared down the hallway with Derrik while Ogden, Seamus, and Lance went the opposite direction, looking at Lance with concern the entire way back to their home. Once they stepped inside, they were immediately greeted by Beatrice eager for news.

"How did the meeting go?" Beatrice asked Ogden, a tinge of hopefulness in her voice.

"Not good. The Elders are taking some extremely drastic measures. They're sending Lance and Shushannah out past the Edge."

"Oh no," Beatrice gasped, putting both hands to her face and looking to Lance who was visibly unphased and had comfortably reclined on the sofa, enjoying the comfort from the cushions far more than the chairs they were forced to sit in before.

Wallais stood in the back of the room quietly chewing his lip looking at his parents, a sign that Ogden and the rest immediately picked up on from past experience trying to keep the two boys out of trouble.

"You wanted this didn't you, Lance?" Ogden asked in disbelief.

"Yeah, I did. Wallais and I were talking about it for a little this morning, but I was going to talk to my mom before doing anything. Seamus heard me talking to Wallais about it and stopped me in the halls before I made it home. Sampson heard us talking and then called the Community meeting."

"What?" Ogden barked, shooting a glare at Seamus, "Why am I Just hearing about this now?"

"He was trying to convince me that it wasn't safe to go out there," Lance reasoned, trying to get Ogden to ease off of Seamus who was now shooting a dagger-filled glare at Lance.

"Why would you want to go out there in the first place? Do you have some sort of death wish?" Ogden interrogated.

"I don't have a death wish, but I can't help but feel like we have an opportunity to find food out there and hiding away behind our walls is only squandering that opportunity. I needed to see for myself to be sure, and today the Elders gave me that opportunity. I think this is the right solution to our problems. This is our last ditch effort to save the Community! To save our families! Don't you want that?"

Ogden took a seat on the couch next to Lance, scratching at his beard roughly.

"I don't know," he said shaking his head repeatedly, "I just don't trust it."

"I know you don't. Nobody does, not even the Elders themselves, but this is something that has to be done. I *hate* killing animals, but I do it anyway because I have a duty to keep the Community fed—to keep my family fed. This is no different from that. Besides, an order from the Elders is absolute, so it isn't like we have a choice in the matter anyways. My mother and I *have* to go out there."

Ogden looked as if he was going to cry. It was the same look his father gave him when he went out on his first hunt all those years ago. He went over to the large man and hugged him tightly, to which Ogden returned, his large face buried in the front of Lance's tattered sweater.

"It's going to be fine guys, I promise," he said to his second family, the people he had grown to love and respect as much as his own biological family. It was promise that he intended to keep.

He felt Ogden pull away and saw him nod, wiping away a stray tear. "I just worry for you and your mother, Little One. I don't want anything to happen to you two. Promise you two will stay safe? Promise you two will return to us?"

"I promise, Ogden. I promise that both my mom and I will return in one piece and hopefully with some good news. But I need to go, I have to let my dad know what's going on before it gets to be too late. I'll be sure to bring my mom by once we speak with the Elders again and we have a concrete plan."

He hugged the remaining members of Wallais's family goodbye before leaving.

He stepped out into the hallway with both hands in his pockets and a smile on his face. He considered himself a lucky person to have this many people in his life that cared this much about him. He knew that this would have to work—it just *had* to. Too much had gone wrong in the Community for this *not* to work out in their favor.

He took the stairs down to the lobby of the Alabaster Rampart two at a time. He looked up just in time to see Jasper and Derrik making their way over to him. He groaned and stood his ground as the pair approached him, Jasper sporting his trademark sneer and Derrik looking lost while he waited for Jasper to take the lead.

"Why is it that I see this little Outsider around here so much, Derrik? It makes me think that he wants to assimilate into Founder life. Someone should tell him that it just isn't in his cards."

Jasper's words were loud—loud enough that a small crowd of people turned to look and then meandered over being familiar with the eventful interactions between the two men. Derrik giggled stupidly beside Jasper. Lance's eyes darted from Jasper to Derrik, watching their movements to make sure they didn't surprise him with anything. He wasn't about to be caught off-guard when he was outnumbered in fight, as his memory served when he would have to peel himself up off of the ground, bloodied when Jasper and his goons jumped him. His fists stayed at his side, but were balled up tightly and were ready to start swinging at a moment's notice.

"What do you want?" Lance hissed.

"I just wanted to wish you luck on your next hunt," Jasper said smugly. Then his voice dropped so only the trio of men could hear it and not the small group that had encircled them waiting for a fight to break out. "You're going to need it. I doubt you're even going to come back." Jasper stood in front of Lance with a satisfied smile, one that he wanted to wipe off of his stupid face by repeatedly smashing it with his fist, but he calmed himself down enough to realize he was yet again being goaded. Maybe Jasper had some smarts after all, Lance almost fell for it this time.

Lance snorted, still keeping both men in his vision. "Fuck off, Jasper. I'm not in the mood for your shit today."

Jasper feigned a stunned gasp, playing the "good friend" for his audience.

"What?" he said with words dripping in sarcasm, "I was just wishing a friend luck is all! People here are counting on you to bring some food back home for us is all! There's no need for such aggressive language!"

Jasper stepped in close before stating the next few words.

"And I'm counting on you not coming back you filthy dirt-dweller."

Lance's eyes widened as a searing rage pumped through his veins. Every atom in his body was screaming at him to pin Jasper down and beat his face into a pulp, but the rational side of his mind broke through the hazy rage and he once again calmed himself down before acting on his emotions. His heavy breathing subsided, and his fists uncurled but he didn't move.

Jasper smirked again.

"C'mon, Derrik. Let's leave him to it. Ta-ta for now, Lance!"

Jasper sauntered off with Derrik in tow, leaving Lance alone in the atrium. The circle of people dispersed, some sighed, while others mumbled to themselves, annoyed that nothing happened.

Ignoring them, he continued on to his cabin. The cold outside air hitting his skin and piercing through his sweater instantly soothed his rage as he then became focused on keeping himself warm for the trek home. He walked in, shaking off the cold, to find everyone sitting around the table, his mother included who looked as if she had just come home herself. They all looked at him, his irritation returning as he thought of Jasper's words. Shushannah still had dirt smudges on her face and stray twigs in her hair.

"What happened to you?" she asked.

"Jasper happened. What about you? You look like you lost a fight with a tree."

She plucked a twig from her hair. "Nothing important, just weaving through some heavy bushes. Your father says you were summoned by the Elders today?"

"Yeah, we need to talk," Lance sighed, taking a seat at the table. Adelade bounded over and he almost told her to go play when he remembered their conversation earlier. She was part of this now and it was going to take some getting used to on his part. She beamed up at him as she rested her chin on the heels of her hands.

"What's up?" Marrick asked, eager to hear the news.

"Well, long story short the Elders gave the order that both Mom and I are to go past the Edge to see if there is any danger out there, but more importantly, if there's food."

Both his mother and father smiled, which made him furrow his brow, confused at their reaction. "You guys aren't concerned or worried? Ogden and all of them damn near had a funeral being planned for us already!"

"Your mother already went out there today. She just got back now," his father explained.

"What?" Lance barked, "You went but didn't take me?! What if something happened?!"

"But it didn't and don't you raise your voice at me! I don't care if you're an adult or not, you're still my damned kid," she fired back.

"Sorry," Lance muttered before continuing, "But how could you do this and not tell us?"

"It wasn't like I was planning to go out there today. I had no luck finding even a trace of a mouse to track and I found myself staring at the Edge. One thing led to another and I just went for it, hoping for the best."

"What is it like out there?" Lance asked, curiosity simmering within his gut.

"It isn't anything special. It's no different from the forest around here. I didn't see any large monsters or sludge puddles or anything like that. It's just grass, air, trees. I didn't go very far, but there's signs of animal life out there. I saw prints, dung, broken twigs, all of it!"

Lance couldn't contain his smile. He would have been lying if he told someone he wasn't nervous to go past the Edge. He was afraid that there was some merit to the words of the Elders, but to find out that, not only is it safe past their borders, but that his hunch about finding more game to hunt made his stomach flutter with excitement.

"I'm surprised you did that. You're never one to break the rules," Lance teased.

"Yeah, well I don't *always* follow the rules," she retorted, "Besides, what would they care if I never came back? They're sending us out there already anyways."

They smiled at each other knowing that there was a light at the end of the tunnel. The answer to their problems was under their noses the whole time. Lance's mind began to wander thinking of all the meals he missed and how he could have had them if they had gone past the Edge earlier, but he pushed the thoughts from his mind. What mattered most was that they were going now and that there was proof that there was game to hunt.

"The Elders said they would send Peter to us in the morning when they were ready to go over a plan with us," Lance explained.

"Okay, but Lance, let's keep my little excursion between us, okay? I don't want the Elders to have a reason to be upset with us. Let's just act like nothing happened for now."

"Alright, Mom. Don't worry about it."

"Good." Her eyes narrowed as she adjusted herself in her seat. "I know I probably don't *have* to ask, but I'm curious. Was it you that volunteered us to be the ones to go past the Edge or were we chosen?"

"What do you think?"

She scoffed in annoyance. "I knew it, those fucking assholes. Send the expendable Outsiders out to die. Worst case scenario we die and and best case they get food for their fat stomachs while they sit around all day. Pricks."

Lance stood up with a groan, feeling every ache in his body, and crossed the room to the wash basin where he splashed water on his face and pulled back his long hair so it wouldn't fall into his eyes. It was still early in the day, but he felt exhausted. He figured he would take it easy and do some reading as tomorrow would be the big day. It would be good to just sit and enjoy some time off knowing that the future was looking good for the first time in ages.

Shushannah followed him over, at which time he plucked twigs from her knotted hair with a chuckle. She snorted with a grin of her own and wiped away the grime from her face.

After cleaning themselves, Lance made himself comfortable for the night and kicked up his feet. The tension he had been carrying around in his shoulders melted away and he woke up the next morning feeling refreshed, albeit hungry as there was again no dinner the night prior, but he hoped that last night would be the last night they had to skip a meal.

A heavy knock at the front door made him jump. Shushannah opened the door, blocking his view of who was there, but the sound of heavy wheezing told him that it was Peter there to summon them to see the Elders. Without hesitation, Lance pulled on his boots and joined his mother at the door, ready to get the day started.

A heavy frost had settled in overnight, crystallizing the yellowing grass. The trio crunched their way across the frozen field at a brisk pace and all the way up to the Chamber of the Elders. When they arrived, they found two chairs placed directly in front of the Elders, the same uncomfortable chairs Lance sat in the day before.

He could already feel his ass going numb.

Both Sampson and Boris were smiling, while Maxwell had a look of devilish intent on his face. Lance had a feeling he was hoping they wouldn't make it back. Lance shot him a glare before sitting down. The fucking asshole.

Lance and Shushannah were barely able to take their seats before Sampson spoke with an excited glimmer in his eyes.

"Good morning, good morning! I will make this brief so we don't waste any more time! Shushannah, I trust that young Lance here has explained the situation to you," she nodded, "Good, good! Then we can all get right to the point! Our plan is to have the both of you map out your journey as you go past the Edge. We trust you two to be able to create a map for the rest of your fellow hunters to follow. You will be doing Community: 1049 a great service! We greatly appreciate you doing this!"

They remained silent, knowing that their "reward" for doing this would be an extra helping of perpetual stew and nothing more.

"We have sent Peter to fetch some supplies from the school room so that you two may draw up the maps. I believe that it goes without saying that we need these maps back quickly and efficiently so that your fellow hunters may assist you in gathering food. As of now, feel free to see yourselves home so that you may head out today to gather your gear and begin documenting. Happy hunting!"

Lance and Shushannah stood up and followed Sampson's gesturing hand to the door and didn't stop until they walked through the front door of their cabin.

Upon entering, Adelade tackled Lance, forcing a puff of hair to escape his mouth. He smiled and held her tight. "You're getting big," he said into the top of her ruffled hair. He wished he hadn't said it. She *was* getting big and she wouldn't be a little kid forever that could leap into his arms to say "Hello". One day she was going to do it for the last time and he wouldn't even realize it.

"Don't break your brother," Marick chuckled from his chair at the table.

"Yeah, I need him to hunt today," Shushannah joked.

"Sorry," Adelade apologized with a sly grin, knowing right well that she would tackle him again before the week was out.

Lance smiled down at her. "Don't worry, you can do that as long as you want. It'll take more than that to break me." He winked at her, which drew a smile to her face before she bounded off.

"So when do you two go out?" Marick asked.

"Once Peter gets here," Shushannah explained, "Evidently we are mapping the area out before anyone else goes out there."

"Did you tell them that you can't draw?" Marick jabbed jokingly.

"Nope, I was just going to make Lance do it."

"Wait, what?" he asked, caught off-guard while counting his arrows. They all laughed but Lance was well aware that he would be the one drawing their path. His mother really *did* have horrible drawing skills. They made little Addie's drawings look like Picasso's.

They split apart to gather their things before Peter arrived. Lance could hear Peter huffing up to their door with mapping supplies in hand before he even knocked. Lance grinned out of sight when Peter appeared in the doorway of their home with rolled papers spilling from his arms and pencils gripped tightly in his hands. He had a panicked look on his face. He scurried in after giving a quick, "Hello," where he dropped the items on the table. Lance straightened his face and turned to thank Peter but he was already gone when he turned to look.

"He never stops does he?" Lance wondered aloud.

"Nope," Marick chuckled, "He's going to have a heart attack before he even reaches mid-adulthood."

Lance saw Adelade moving to the table from the corner of his eye. Her hands were outstretched and her eyes were as big as two moons. He snatched the papers up before she could get her greedy little hands on them.

"Nope, not for you kid," he said, casually tossing the rolls to his mother who stuffed them into her bag.

"Aw, please just one?"

"We'll get you more later," Marick compromised, "Your Mom and brother need those papers for their maps."

"Aw, okay," she mumbled as she shuffled away to her corner and flopped down on her bundle of blankets with a huff.

"Life is so hard," Lance noted to his parents sarcastically with a grin.

He shouldered his bow and quiver, redirecting his attention to the matter at hand. He made sure his boot-knife was strapped in tightly and looked to his mother to see her loading the last of the pencils into her bag. She already had her bow and arrows on her shoulder and her hair tied up in a tight bun. They said their goodbyes to Adelade and Marick before setting off.

They ventured into the woods, taking the well-worn dirt path they had been taking to their usual hunting grounds for years. Lance could have walked it with his eyes closed.

He waited until they were a good distance away from the Community before striking up a conversation with his mother.

"Did you happen to catch Maxwell's face earlier?" Lance asked, the thought gnawing at the back of his mind the entirety of the morning.

"I did, but is it really anything new? He was probably hoping we would get eaten by a bear. Then his little bastard son can take all the glory when he brings home food."

"Makes sense."

"Plus the shit you and Jasper keep getting into must aggravate him too. It's unbecoming to see a leader who can't control his own son."

"He's an adult, Jasper should be able to control himself."

"Like you did a few weeks ago with Tim," she teased.

He rolled his eyes.

"How far did you go out yesterday?" he asked, desperate to change the subject. He wanted to forget about the whole thing with Timothy and the rancid bathrooms he spent a week of his life much too close and personal with.

"Not very. I didn't want to get lost and I wasn't sure what was out there. There's another set of woods a short distance away that showed signs of animals in the area, but I didn't see any while I was out there. We may get lucky today and find some. Especially since you're mapping the area out, we can go out a lot farther."

Lance sighed, a puff of steam coming from his nostrils, remembering that he would be drawing instead of really being able to take in the new scenery. "You should probably give me the paper and pencils then. They won't do me any good in your bag."

Shushannah stopped, pulling her rucksack off of her shoulder and opened it. She pulled out the now crumpled papers with a couple pencils. Lance took them, folding the papers into squares so they would be stiff enough to draw on. He pocketed the pencils for now and followed behind Shushannah who had continued on without him.

They didn't speak until they reached the clearing at the end of the treeline where they stopped. Lance could feel his excitement rising in his chest. He had never been this close to the Edge before, and yet here he was about to cross it and make history in the Community. He wondered if this was how his mother felt yesterday.

She turned to face him, a stern look on her face.

"Now, even though you're mapping this area out, keep on your toes. If there is an animal, I don't care if it's a mouse, you take it down. I don't want to hear any of this 'didn't need to' bullshit from you. This map isn't an excuse not to bring home food for our people."

Lance gritted his teeth. He locked eyes with his mother, refusing to look away.

"I'll do what needs to be done. I'm not a child and you don't need to tell me what to do."

"I'm just making sure you understand the importance of this," she grumbled, looking away and adjusting her bag.

Lance furrowed his brow, wondering where the sudden agitation came from. He ignored it, chalking it up to her being stressed about the food situation. He had to admit, he wasn't the most diligent hunter in the past, but the situation was different. He knew he had to put his reservations aside or else people were going to die. He readied a pencil and stood beside his mother.

"Ready?" she asked, not breaking her gaze from the treeline.

"Ready."

"Let's go then."

Holding his breath, Lance took a step forward, his first step past the Edge and into a whole new world.

7

Lance furiously drew on the paper, being sure to note important landmarks for his fellow hunters to follow, such as oddly shaped rocks or dead trees laying in different formations. On occasion, he or Shushannah would carve a diamond-shaped mark into the bark of a tree with their knives if there were no landmarks to be seen.

They were mostly silent as they traveled, occasionally pointing out a pile of scat or broken branches indicating that an animal had been in the area. The signs were there, but the animals however were not, which slightly depressed Lance.

He had been doing well mapping out the area around them and Shushannah would occasionally check in on him to be sure that he was documenting their progress correctly. She had very little to point out about his maps, and what little she did bring up were only suggestions to help make the maps a little easier for everyone else to follow.

The pair had been walking for only a couple of hours, and much to Lance's disdain, they didn't stumble upon any Old World structures. It was mostly wooded, which had admittedly brought Lance's mood down slightly. Part of his excitement to go past the Edge was to explore and see ruins from the old world. He had seen how the people of the past lived in books he read over the years, but to see it in person would be a whole different experience. He wondered what it would be like to watch television—to so see a figure moving on those electronic boxes. He imagined what it would be like to drive in a car or take a girl on a date to the movies. He wished that the people of the Old World appreciated what they had and took care of it because now it had all gone to shit. Generation upon generation missed out on so many things, himself included, because of the callous lack of care by the human race's ancestors.

"Want to take a break?" Shushannah asked, interrupting Lance's internal rant.

"Sure," he agreed, noting that his feet were beginning to hurt and his hand was cramping.

He sat down against the rough trunk of a large oak tree, the cold earth immediately freezing his legs and ass. He reviewed the map, his finger tracing their path to see how far they traveled. They covered at least eight miles and the sun was still high in the sky. He assumed that they would be able to go a little longer before having to head back to the Community.

"I can't believe we haven't found a damn thing out here still," his mother sighed, sitting against a tree of her own just across from Lance and looking up at the gray sky.

"We will. We keep seeing signs that there's life out here, and it's only a matter of time before something crosses our path."

"I hate going home empty-handed."

Lance produced a frown, not knowing what to say to his mother to help her feel better. It was tough for him when his mother opened up like this as he could never figure out the best way to give comfort to her. When he tried, no matter the method, she would always brush him off in irritation. He learned that it was best to just let her speak her mind and leave it at that.

"How much longer do you think we should stay out here for?" he asked.

"I suppose we could turn back soon. I'd rather not be out here in the dark. We aren't familiar with this place like we are with the forest around the Community. Spending the night out here could be bad. Plus, we need to report back to the Elders."

"It looks like it should be a little after noontime, so we should have maybe another four to five hours of sunlight left I believe."

"I say let's keep going another hour and turn back. We can walk in a different direction tomorrow so that we can have a wider area mapped out."

"Sounds good to me."

Shushannah turned her gaze to a dried stick lying on the ground next to her. She absentmindedly pulled the stick into her hands and began breaking it into little pieces. She had a neutral expression on her face as she stared off into nothing, obviously lost among her own thoughts. She was gone to the world for the moment.

He allowed himself to enjoy the break for a while longer, longing for the days of Spring to return where there would be some color in the world again other than the drab tones of gray and brown that took over as everything either died or went dormant for the upcoming Winter months. The air around him was dead and silent except for the wind rushing past his exposed ears, numbing them, as the birds and the bugs fled to warmer climates until it was warm enough to return.

He wished he could follow them there.

"Let's get going, we're losing daylight," Shushannah announced, standing up and breaking out of her trance.

Lance followed, scrambling to his feet and ready to move on and warm up his body. His leather overcoat wasn't helping much, but it was better than nothing.

The pair continued on their way for another twenty minutes or so before his mother grabbed him roughly by the shoulder.

"Lance," she breathed excitedly, "Look!"

He followed her pointed finger through the bare trees and saw what made her so excited. He could see a structure in the distance that looked like the corner of a roof. He eagerly scribbled down their position as they half-jogged, half-walked towards the dwelling, seeing it for what it really was. Lance made sure to draw a crude house with an excited grin before pocketing the paper and pencil to explore the house with his mother. Upon drawing closer to the structure, they realized that they were standing in the backyard of the house.

The house stood two-stories tall with a dense net of brown vines clinging to the rotted siding that struggled to stay above the puckered earth below as it was being dragged down underneath to its inevitable grave. Faded pink sheets of paint dangled in the breeze from the sides of the house that Lance assumed was once red in color, though was bleached from decades of weathering and sun exposure. Jutting through the waist-high grass, he could just make out the remains of a small, jagged, picket fence that was only barely standing with a couple of weak pickets covered in moss and stripped of their paint that were waiting for one final gust of wind to push them down where they would join the other pickets that had long since rotted into the soil below. Most of the windows were broken, with shards of glass sticking up through the dry-rotted window panes. Those that weren't broken were marred with a thick grime that blocked the view of the interior.

As they waded through grass, Lance tripped over something solid. He bent down to untangle the object from the grass to find a heavily rusted hunk of metal. There were three wheels on it that were completely rusted over with dry-rotted rubber barely clinging to what he deduced to be a rim. The plastic seat bolted to the frame was crusted over with dirt and bleached of color. It had small cracks covering its surface with one large crack cutting directly through the center where the rusted bolt had stained the surrounding plastic brown. He recognized what he was holding as a tricycle, though it was beyond use as the two pedals on the trike were so heavily rusted that he couldn't get them to rotate. He smiled, thinking of how a toddler may have ridden the little bike around, experiencing the excitement of having their own bike, something that he never had the chance to experience. He dropped it back into the grass with a frown and a silent curse at his ancestors.

He followed his mother around to the front of the house. There was a dirt road in front of the house, but there were no other houses that he could see nearby. He did however manage to see a smaller shed nearby that was hidden by the side of the house that piqued his curiosity to see what was inside.

The front of the house was in far worse shape than the back, as all the windows had been shattered and the vines cascading down the sides were thicker, though just as dead as the ones wrapping the back of the house. There was a massive hole in the roof where the end of a fallen tree limb had crashed through and what remained of the roof was covered in a thick blanket of dried moss. Another tree limb stuck out from the windows on the right side and where a front door should be was just empty space leading inside. The interior was too dark to see inside from where they stood, so he couldn't see what was just beyond the doorway to the house. Leading up to the front door was a pathway of stones that were just barely visible from the puckering earth below, which he estimated would be fully submerged under the grass within the decade.

As they made their way up to the house, Lance could smell the water-logged interior before they even stepped inside. As they stepped over the threshold, Lance saw the splintered and rotted remains of the front door on the weather-beaten wooden floor.

As he stepped through the doorway, he felt the floor buckle under his boot. He stopped and looked back at his mother. "Careful," he muttered before taking another step. As he went in farther, the floor was in better shape, but not by much. The surface of the floorboards were stripped down to raw, splintered wood from where debris from the woods skidded through from years of heavy winds, rain, snow and the like. A black fungus had spread over the ceiling, prompting Lance and Shushannah to pull their undershirts over their faces. He looked around more, seeing a decimated television in the corner of the room with plants growing happily out of the shattered screen. More plants were jutting up through the cracks of the floorboards in various spots from where seeds were brought in through the broken windows. A couch sat in front of the television with brittle, dirt-encrusted fabric that he could push his finger through with little to no effort. He wiped the grime away on his pants with disgust.

He made an attempt to climb up the stairs, but the first one collapsed immediately before he could put his full weight on his foot. He slowly backed away, the structural integrity of the house clearly in question.

"Let's look back here," Shushannah offered, pointing around to a hallway that looked like it led to more rooms.

He followed behind her, peering into each of the three rooms in the hallway. They were basic bedrooms, nothing all that different from the ones back at the Community in The Alabaster Rampart. There were broken tables and dressers, as if someone had come in and destroyed everything. The beds were in shambles, what remained of the sheets were brittle strips of fabric on moth-eaten mattresses. He opened each closet, finding them bare. The final room of the three was a bathroom with a stained toilet and broken sink. The tile flooring was crumbled and smelled of severe water damage like the rest of the house.

It was all a big disappointment.

"I hope all the houses aren't all like this," he uttered.

"There's a good chance that they are. It's been decades since anyone has set foot in places like these. I bet this house is in better shape than most since it's sheltered by the trees."

He frowned, deciding that it was best to just leave the house while it was still standing. He was sure to step over the rotting floor before finding himself back outside with his mother. He made sure to mark on the map that the house was unsafe with a disappointed sigh before they continued on their way.

He hoped to himself that they could find a house that was safe to stay inside for more than five minutes so he could do some actual exploring.

"Hey what's that?" Shushannah asked, pointing to a tree.

Lance looked to where she was pointing and saw a strange symbol carved into the bark. It looked as if it had been carved a few days prior as the fresh bark underneath had since dried and was beginning to gray slightly. He craned his neck to get a better look at the curious carving. It looked like an eye that had been crossed out.

"I didn't do that. I don't know what that is."

They looked at each other and then looked around, readying their bows.

They were not alone out here.

"We need to get back to the Community," Shushannah whispered.

"Yeah," Lance breathed, his pulse rising with his anxiety.

The pair broke into a light jog, minding the map that Lance drew up to find their way back. He hoped that he did a good job as he couldn't remember their surroundings as they quickly made their way back home. As they darted through the trees, they glanced around them to be sure they weren't being followed. Lance hated the feeling of being chased, thinking of all the times he chased down animals in the past to finish them off. It was as if the universe was ironically punishing him for it.

After about twenty minutes, they stopped dead in their tracks as two figures stepped out in front of them from behind a pair of trees.

Before them stood two shirtless men brandishing sharp machete blades and malicious grins. Lance froze as his mind feebly tried to process the men standing before him. The skin on their bodies was heavily scarred. One of the men was missing his right eye and most of the hair on his scalp. He was smiling, revealing a row of rotted, yellow teeth. The other man was sporting a long beard but a large scar stretched from the top of his right shoulder, across his chest, and down into his raggedy trousers. Despite the cold, they didn't seem fazed at all by it. It was as if they were *proud* to display their scars.

To Lance, not only just seeing these mutilated people froze him in place, but the fact that there was anyone even *alive* out here. The Elders had told them for years that Community: 1049 were the only surviving humans left on the planet, yet, here were two standing before him and his mother.

"You two are trespassing on land belonging to the Tested," the man missing an eye announced with a voice deep and gravely, "You two seem to be a bit far from home."

The bearded man chuckled as they split apart, circling around Lance and Shushannah, taking slow steps. Her bow was raised, as was Lance's, but they didn't let their nocked arrows go. Sweat was forming on Lance's brow. He adjusted his footing, keeping the bearded man in his sights while the one-eyed man went to his right, out of his own line of sight but still within his mother's. He surmised that there must be more of them out here somewhere. He shuddered at the thought, wondering if they were nearby.

"Let us pass," Shushannah spoke, her voice steady and confident.

"No," Lance heard the one-eyed man say.

Lance's back was pressed against his mothers as both men had spread out even farther now. They had stopped for the moment, or at least the bearded man did, with his machete swinging at his side. He had a wild grin on his face and Lance had the sinking feeling in his gut that the man either didn't care about getting shot with an arrow or he was *excited* by the idea of it.

"It's dangerous in these parts of the woods," the bearded man spoke now, his voice higher than Lance expected, "We'll make sure you get home safely. Where's your camp?"

Lance's arms were getting tired but he didn't dare release the tension in his shoulders.

"None of your business," Shushannah barked over her shoulder, "We can take care of ourselves, we don't need an escort."

"But you do," the one-eyed man said, his voice dripping in sarcasm now, "And when we bring you home safely, you can reward us."

"We aren't giving you shit," she spat, "And we *certainly* won't be going anywhere with you two."

Lance began to worry about everyone back home. He set his jaw and made sure his aim was true.

Both men laughed. The bearded man took a single step towards

Lance and stopped. He cocked his head to the side, and with his left hand, pointed directly at his heart. Lance swallowed a lump down and licked sweat from his lips. He refused to blink and made absolutely sure that the man was in line of fire. He kept telling himself in his mind that it was him or them, that killing the man was no different from killing a deer or rabbit. It had to be done.

"Where is your camp?" the other man asked, this time with more conviction in his voice. Lance could hear snapping twigs behind him as the one-eyed man inched closer. The bearded man remained still, his finger still lingering on his chest, daring Lance to shoot him.

"I'm not telling you a thing," Shushannah said flatly.

"Then we'll kill you and have the boy show us the way."

Lance's stomach dropped hearing this. These two men were clearly deranged, between the lack of clothing in the freezing temperatures, the scarring of their bodies, and the way they spoke, it scared Lance thinking about what they could do to the people he loved. There was no way out of this except to fight their way out. If he missed his shot, he needed to be ready to dodge the machete when it came swinging for him.

"So be it," Shushannah muttered.

Before Lance was able to release his arrow, one had already pierced the bearded man's neck from the left, spraying blood from the struck artery. The machete fell as the man's hands found their way up, groping uselessly at the arrow jutting from his neck, at which time the man fell to his knees, his smile gone, and then proceeded to flop face down into the dirt unmoving. Lance turned after stepping away from his mother to see that she had already shot the other man dead on the spot as he lay lifeless on his back with an arrow sticking straight up from the center of his forehead and a look of shock on his face.

Lance looked around the forest for the shooter of the other arrow, at which time a woman stepped out from behind a tree, aiming her own bow at both Lance and Shushannah.

"Put down your weapons now or I'll drop both of you where you stand," she ordered.

Shushannah turned, bewildered to the girl, while at the same time Lance lowered his bow as he was sure she would hit him from where she was before he could even turn his aim to her.

She looked different from the two men that were now lying dead on the forest floor. She was fully clothed for one, and didn't appear to be sporting any of those nasty scars on her body. She had black hair pulled back into a ponytail and what appeared to be brown eyes, though Lance was more interested in the loaded bow she had pointed at him. She had the perfect stance for an archer and a body that looked like it could move gracefully through the woods. She was built like a hunter which meant she could shoot like a hunter.

Slowly, Lance lowered his bow to the ground and put both of his hands up in the air.

"You too, lady," the girl barked, "Bow on the ground now."

Lance could hear a slight growl rumble in Shushannah's throat, but she complied with the unknown girl.

Without taking her eyes off both Lance and his mother, she stomped up to both of them and stopped about seven feet or so away. Her eyes were darting from Lance to his mother and back to him again. Her fingers were steady and she showed no signs of wavering confidence, unlike Lance whose mouth was wide open and his chest was sucking in heavy gulps of air as his heart hammered away in his ears. Fist fights were one thing, but his life was on the line here. He didn't know what to do.

"Who are you two? Where are you from?" the woman asked.

"Around," Shushannah answered, her anger coming through gritted teeth.

"Well, around where? Neither one of you are carrying more than a day's worth of gear, obviously you have a camp somewhere. How many of you are there?"

"Enough of us to get by," Shushannah answered again.

The woman was getting irritated. She pointed the nocked arrow at Shushannah who remained unphased.

"I'll ask one more time and then this arrow is going right between your fucking eyes."

Shushannah didn't speak and only maintained eye contact with the woman, her jaw set in place. Lance stood, rooted in his spot and not knowing what to do. His mother was going to get herself killed if she didn't comply. He opened his mouth to speak and then thought better of it. He forgot about the people back home. Who knows what could happen if this woman found out where they live? What could happen to Adelade? To Marick? To Wallais and his family? His mother was right to protect them.

He balled his fists and mentally prepared himself. He had to be fast if he was going to get to the woman. He hoped that he could get to her before she could aim her bow anywhere deadly, and if she did, that it didn't hit something too important, or better yet, *missed.*

"Don't think about it," she muttered from the corner of her mouth to Lance, "I'll drop you before you even take a step. If you two haven't noticed, I saved both of your asses. The least you could do is be a little more polite."

"W-who were those people?" Lance asked, trying to just make sense of the chaos in front of him.

"The Tested. They're a group of nasty people that mutilate themselves to prove their loyalty to their leader, Bastion. They must have been following you two for quite some time."

"Are there more around here?" Shushannah asked, looking around and temporarily forgetting about the woman with the aimed bow.

"Most likely. They travel in packs. You never answered my questions and now I've answered two of yours. *Who are you two?*"

"I'm Lance. This is my mom, Shushannah."

"My name is Rosalie. Now my other question, where do you two live?"

"We have family there, we aren't likely to divulge that information to you," Shushannah said flatly. She would not be budging and Rosalie seemed to understand that too.

"If I lower my bow you two promise not to attack me?"

"I promise," Lance said looking over to his mother.

"Yeah, fine," she muttered.

Rosalie lowered her bow and replaced the arrow into the quiver on her back. She kept her distance, still wary, but altogether less on edge. Lance got a better look at her now that she wasn't waving around a weapon. She had well-worn clothing on with patches of random fabric sewn on in places. He guessed her pants were once a pair of jeans, but were now more patch-worked fabric than jeans. She had on a pair of boots with a leather jacket and ripped up hoodie, though it still appeared to be functional enough.

"We need to find a place to sleep for the night," she stated, "You two would do well to follow me for now. If there's more of them out there, you're as good as dead."

Lance wasn't about to take that chance, especially if they followed him and Shushannah back to the Community. He looked to his mother who had a stern look cemented on her face. He silently pleaded for her to just this one time not to be so hard-headed. She finally met his gaze and nodded. He let out a small trapped breath. "Yeah, we'll follow. Do you have some place nearby?"

"Oh, so you guys want to know where *I* live but I don't get to know where *you* live."

"It's not like that—," Lance started, but was stopped when Rosalie raised a hand and grinned.

"It's fine, I'm only fucking with you. I'm not taking you to my people either, I'm sure you understand. There's a place nearby we can crash for the night and make sure you two aren't being followed. Then we can go out separate ways and pretend this never happened. Deal?"

"Deal," Lance agreed, eagerly wanting to hurry and get out of the open and into shelter.

"Then let's go and try to keep up," she said turning on her heel and breaking into a jog.

They darted through the trees, stopping now and then for Rosalie to determine the next turn to take. It took them about a half an hour to find the little one-story house Rosalie was leading them to. It was in decent shape, but not much different from the other house they saw earlier. At least this one had a roof, as old and untrustworthy as it was. If it stood this long, it would at least make it through the night.

Rosalie pushed open the door, her bow drawn and cleared the rooms. Once they were sure it was safe, they closed the door and huddled down in a corner. The windows of this house were smashed in here too, and Lance realized the glass was inside on the floor a bit too late when he felt a sting on his palm. He sighed in agitation and plucked the glass from his hand, tossing it off to the side. He wasn't bleeding badly so he ignored the cut for now. He would clean it tomorrow when he got home.

The house smelled like the other one, dry-rotted and dusty with a slight hint of something long dead and decayed. He didn't care for the smell at all, but he would stomach it for the night in exchange for a safe place to rest.

They were all seated on the floor as there was no furniture in the house, not even broken furniture. It looked as if it had been abandoned or completely looted years ago.

"You two must not be from around here," Rosalie spoke, cutting the silence, "Everyone around here knows the Tested, knows their symbol. It means 'off-limits'. Where are you two from?"

Lance and Shushannah exchanged a glance. Rosalie wouldn't drop the subject anytime soon, but she seemed safe enough to reveal their home to. If she meant them any harm, she would have let those two men kill them instead of saving them.

"We live in a Community, established in the Old World," Lance explained.

"Whoa, no shit? Those are still around? I thought they had all collapsed ages ago. How are you guys still functioning? Do you have electricity? Running water?"

Lance shook his head grimly. "We have power and water, yes, but we're on the verge of starving to death. That's why we're out here. There's no more food in the forest surrounding our compound and we're starving. Our numbers are too large and our indoor growing system doesn't work anymore since the soil is out of nutrients."

"I'm surprised that your home hasn't been found yet."

"We were under the impression that we were the last people on the planet," Shushannah interrupted.

"On the *planet*? Who told you that crock of shit? There's plenty of us around here. Sometimes *too many* to be honest."

"Our leaders, the Elders," Shushannah explained, "They told us for years that we were the only ones left. They lost contact with the other Communities before Lance here was born. We never knew there were people out here. We had been hunting in the woods in the area for years and never ran into anyone."

"Where exactly is this Community located?" Rosalie asked, her eyes narrowed.

Lance handed over the map he was drawing to Rosalie. She looked it over and then chuckled to herself. "Of course," she muttered, "You're people are settled in a highly polluted area. Even the Tested don't go near here because there's nothing out there. Evidently that's not the case. You all may just be nuttier than those freaks living out there all this time."

Lance got to his knees and peered out of the broken window. The sun was just clinging to the horizon now. He hoped that Adelade and Marick weren't too worried about him and his mother. They had never spent a night out of the Community before. He wished he could contact them somehow, but knew it was best to wait until morning. They would leave at first light and get back home to their family as soon as they could. He returned to sitting on the floor with a sigh.

"Do you see anything?" Rosalie asked.

He shook his head. "No, nothing."

"You know, I have to ask you two, how did you *not* know you were being followed?"

Lance shrugged. He thought of the chair in the Chamber of the Elders as his ass was going numb again. Even that would be better than the hard floor.

"We're normally the ones *doing* the stalking, not the ones *being* stalked. We don't have much practice with it," his mother said.

"You two better learn to pick up on that if you're going to be hunting out here. You're lucky you ran into me and not someone else."

"You never told us where you lived," Shushannah noted, changing the subject. Lance stifled a grin, his mother didn't like being told when she was bad at something.

"No, I didn't," Rosalie said plainly, stopping for a moment and then continuing, "You two better not be cannibals or some shit." After another brief pause followed by a sigh she continued. "I live in an abandoned mill with my family and a handful of other people. We move around a lot, depending on the Tested, but we generally stay in the area."

"Why not move out of the area completely? Why stick around if these guys are here?" Lance asked.

"There's always been a reason not to. When you have a small group of people such as the three of us, it's easier to move and stay quiet, but when that number grows and you add in little kids, sick people, old people if they're still around, it gets tricky. Moving around as much as we do is a problem in itself. Less and less of us make it each time. Most of us would die if we made a big move. Besides, the Tested have spread out a lot farther than you'd think."

They were silent, Lance began picking a hangnail he noticed, Shushannah just sat stone-like while Rosalie was staring up and out of the broken window pane to see if there were any other Tested coming for them. Lance was still trying to process the day's events. The fact that there were people out here was more than enough shock, but being dangerous people added to the sheer weight of it all. They would return home tomorrow empty handed, but they would have plenty of knowledge to give to the Elders.

He pulled out his map, noting the path that they took to this little house and looked to see how far from home they were. If they left right at sunrise, he figured they could get back to the Community by mid-afternoon at the latest. Maybe they could fit in some hunting on their way back, assuming they weren't being chased by maniacs again.

"Do you think those were the only two Tested?" Lance asked Rosalie.

"At this point, I'm thinking probably. It isn't like them to lie and wait to attack. They just go for it. I wouldn't let your guard down, but I think we're safe for the time being," Rosalie replied.

Lance let out a breath of relief and proceeded to lie down on his back, his arms crisscrossed behind his head to make a pillow. He stared up at the ceiling, bubbles of paint were tearing away from the surface, but it was better than nothing. It was better than being out there where anything could happen to him after all. He was beginning to doubt that it was a good idea to come out here.

It took him a while to close his eyes. He still felt like he could feel eyes on him, but when he would look at either Rosalie or his mother, both of their backs were turned. He would reluctantly peek through the window on occasion, half-expecting to see a face looking back at him, but he saw nothing each time. At one point in the night, he fell asleep but he was unsure when, as he suddenly woke up with a jerk and the sun was up, blinding him through the windows. He looked around, panicked because he didn't see his mother or Rosalie, but calmed down when he saw his mother walk past the window, stretching and waking up herself.

He scrubbed his hair roughly in his hands and pulled on his gear. It felt heavier than yesterday, but he figured his muscles were still trying to recover. He wanted to get home to his blankets and burrow himself inside of them for a week. He missed his blankets.

"About time, we were about to leave you," Shushannah poked.

Lance retorted with a sarcastic laugh. "I couldn't sleep at all last night."

"I don't think any of us did," Rosalie said coming from around the back of the house. Her hair was up in a ponytail like yesterday, "I think we should be fine. You two were lucky that it was only two Tested that pulled away from the pack. There's no sign that any more of them followed us back here, though the fact that we're still alive says more than anything. Thank you for not killing me last night by the way."

Shushannah grunted and adjusted her bag.

Lance pulled the crumpled map from his pocket and made note of their location, trying to find the direction towards home.

"Let me see that," Rosalie asked.

Lance handed her the map. She looked it over and then looked at him. She plucked the pencil from his hands and scribbled something on the map. While she did so, he took a curious peek at her eyes. They were brown after all.

"Here, if you two ever find yourselves lost or in need of help, the mill where I live is here." She handed Lance back the map and pointed. It was a crude, yet understandable drawing she had done. The little factory she drew with a smiling face just above it was about 6 miles or so North from the house they found yesterday.

"Thank you," Lance said, surprised she would give them her home location.

"I figure if I know where you live that it's only fair that you know where I live."

"We appreciate it," Shushannah interjected, "We really should be going though, Marick is no doubt worried about us and we have a lot of ground to cover to get back home."

"Yeah, I do too," Rosalie agreed, "Be safe, and make sure to look around once and awhile. Remember, you guys aren't the only hunters out here."

"We will. You be safe too. Let's go, Lance."

Lance waved goodbye to Rosalie before following his mother in the opposite direction, back towards home. He was sure it was the events from the day prior making him paranoid, but he couldn't shake the feeling that they were being watched the whole way back to the Community. His senses were on high alert, and every snapping twig or rustling pile of leaves made him pause to look around. He could tell that his mother was getting annoyed with him, but he ignored her. He wasn't about to allow them to get caught by surprise again.

It was well past noontime when the pair finally stumbled back into the Community. They were both exhausted and in need of rest. Their first stop was home, where an exhausted looking Marick greeted them both with a tight hug. Adelade was next, tears running down her face and blubbering madly about how she thought they were dead. They calmed her down and explained their night out in the woods. It wasn't long before there was a knock at the door.

Marick opened the door to reveal Peter with his usual sweaty face.

"The Elders are requesting the presence of Lance and Shushannah," he huffed.

"Of course they are," Shushannah sighed, "Not even a fucking minute to catch our breath."

Lance stood up, feeling as if he slept on a rock and made his way over to the door. He looked back at Adelade, and after casting her a big smile, he said, "Be back soon, kid," before closing the door behind him.

8

Lance flopped himself down in the chair once he and his mother walked into the Chamber of the Elders. He felt like he hadn't slept in days and his body felt like it was encased in cement. Every step he took used all his willpower. Hell, even just standing was a chore at this point. He just wanted to go home and sleep already.

Elder Sampson was not as excited to see Lance and his mother as he was yesterday. He looked as if he were in pain or deep thought, though it was difficult for Lance to decipher which. Perhaps the Elders were finally experiencing what hunger pains felt like for the first time. Lance was so used to them now that he hardly noticed them anymore or the persistent rumbles vibrating from his stomach.

He rubbed the stinging tiredness away from his eyes roughly with the palms of his hands and gave a great yawn. He slouched down in his chair and waited for the Elders to begin their line of questioning, ready to get things over with so he could go home and sleep for the next week.

"I see you have returned from your trip empty-handed," Sampson announced with a disappointed sigh. There was Lance's answer.

Lance allowed his mother to answer.

"Yes, we ran into some *very* unexpected trouble," she began.

"What sort of trouble?" Sampson pressed as the Elders all leaned forward at the same time, completely intrigued by what Shushannah was about to say next.

She spoke with a somber tone. "There are other people out there—people that wanted to kill us. They stalked us like we were a couple of deer."

All three Elders gasped and looked at each other in bewilderment. Lance had never seen them act like this before. He noted their surprise to himself, believing that they truly had no knowledge of what was going on past the Edge. He fixed his posture and brought his attention back to the room instead of his bundle of blankets patiently waiting for him at home. Things were about to get interesting.

"We were stalked through the woods by two men part of a larger group called 'The Tested'. We were saved by a woman named Rosalie who has a group of her own."

"Did this woman say how many of these "Tested" people there are? Or how many people are in her own group? Did she say how they were able to survive out there?"

"No. The only information she gave us is that she lives in an old mill or a factory but we didn't get any specifics. We were more concerned about the men hiding in the trees instead of giving her the third degree."

Shushannah proceeded to give the Elders a full recount of the entire night they spent out beyond the Edge. The Elders sat in silence without moving a muscle as Shushannah gave them every detail that she could. When she was finished, Sampson's shoulders were sunken and it seemed as if all hope had fled from his body. He sat back in his chair while Borris and Maxwell looked to him to see what he was planning to do next.

Sampson was silent for a moment before looking to his compatriots and composed himself. They had a silent conversation with each other before Sampson addressed Lance and Shushannah again.

"We will not have you two return out there again. We cannot risk these 'Tested' you speak of finding our home. If they are aware that we are here they will undoubtedly come for us and take this place away from us, and with everything we have going on, this is the last thing we need."

"Sirs, please, we must go back out there. There are clear signs of animal life! I think that proof is enough to outweigh the potential dangers," Shushannah argued.

"No, Shushannah, it is not. Where would our Community be if it is burnt to the ground?"

"Do you not think it will collapse anyway if we all starve to death? What would it matter then? I would rather take the risk to save our people from starvation." Her voice was calm and steady, but Lance could see a small vein in her temple sticking out slightly the same one that swelled with blood when she was on the verge of blowing her top.

"You forget your place, Shushannah. *We* make the decisions for the Community, not *you*. We will continue to hunt in our immediate forest and that is final."

Sampson's words hung in the air, thick and heavy.

"You may leave us. Go home to your family and rest," he commanded with a dismissive wave of his hand. "And please," he added, "Keep this conversation between us for now."

Without speaking, the pair stood from their chairs and shuffled out of the room, feeling more defeated than ever and just wanting to just get a good, safe, night's sleep. They walked into their home and nothing needed to be said to Marick and Adelade to know that the meeting did not provide the results they were looking for. Despite the sun still being up, both Lance and Shushannah collapsed into their beds and were soon heard snoring by both Marick and Adelade who decided to take a walk for a while and let the two rest.

Lance slept well through the rest of the afternoon and into the late hours of the following morning just before noon. He forced his body into a sitting position and peered around him with one eye still closed and the other half open and blurry, trying to determine if he was really home or if he was having a vivid dream. He managed to get his other eye open and sat for a minute waiting for his brain to wake up a bit more. He eventually stood up and stretched, his back cracking in ripples from his lower spine up to his shoulders as he let out a groan of pleasure. He pulled back his curtain and heard the dull snore of his mother behind her own closed curtain. He stepped into his boots and scrubbed his hair down as he walked outside, shivering against the cold air.

"Well good morning," he heard his father say. He was walking back to their cabin, most likely coming back from a walk. He had been taking them more and more lately since the grow rooms had been closed down. He said that they kept him from going stir crazy.

"Morning," he grumbled in reply.

They returned to the inside of the cabin where it was warmer, though not by much. Shushannah was awake when they reentered, he figured she was probably woken up by the door closing when Lance went outside. She looked exhausted still despite sleeping for almost an entire day. She was splashing water on her face when they walked in.

"Take a seat," she said through dabbing a rag on her face. The tone in her voice meant business.

They did as commanded and waited for her to join them.

"We need to be prepared for whatever comes next," she said gravely, "I don't know what the hell the Elders are thinking right now after the information we gave them. I know for sure that they're going to call a meeting, but what information they're going to share with the rest of the Community is up in the air. We need to be prepared for the worst case scenario here."

"I agree," Lance chimed in.

"Same here," Marick noted, though his voice was lacking the same confidence that Lance's and Shushannah's had.

"Good. Then I don't know about you two, but I think no matter what the Elders say, we need to keep going beyond the Edge. Lance, you know just as well as me that we aren't grasping on threads here.

There's solid proof out there that there's animals just waiting for us to find them. I'm thinking the reward outweighs the risk in this situation. I can't watch you all waste away when there's something that we can do about it. It would be different if we didn't see anything out there except for the Tested, but there's also *good* people out there. Not *everything* wants to kill us."

Lance rubbed the stubble on his chin as he dwelled on Shushannah's proposition. It was risky, sure, but he had to admit that he felt the same way. He couldn't just sit around letting his sister starve to death or others he cared about, if there was something he could do to prevent it—the Tested be damned.

He looked his mother dead in the eye with his jaw set. "I'm with you on this," he said confidently.

They both looked to Marick now as he was the deciding vote. He sat back in his chair and put up his hands. "Fine, yeah, do it. I know you two inside and out. There's no stopping either of you, but I'll just say this: when you two didn't come back the other night, I didn't know what Adelade and I were going to do. I didn't know what I was going to tell her. I didn't know how we were going to get by. This is going to be the hardest Winter the Community has seen yet, and we both need you two to get by. If you're going to go out there, please be careful, and *please* come home."

"We will, Dad," Lance soothed, putting a confident hand on his father's shoulder, "We'll be safe and we'll be careful. We came home yesterday, and I can promise you that we'll do it again."

"Yes," Shushannah interjected, "We're going to make sure we have a plan in place before we go back out there. I don't want us to get taken by surprise again like that. Do you still have the map, Lance?"

"I do. The Elders never took it."

"Good, we're going to need it and we're going to add to it too. Why don't you go and get it and we can start planning now? I'd rather have something in place now instead of having to scramble later. It should give us some time to work out any kinks."

Lance retrieved the map from his corner of the cabin and spread it out on the table. Over the course of the next hour or so the trio discussed the best possible methods for Lance and Shushannah to go out and come back into the Community safely. They took some time out of each day for the next week or so to do this, being sure to also include Adelade in the discussion so that she could learn properly for the future. Lance could tell that his little sister was apprehensive to him and his mother going back out, but she kept on a brave face. He was sure to spend extra time with her as much as he could to hopefully put her a little more at ease when he would inevitably go back out.

While they anxiously waited for the Elders to call a meeting over the next couple of days, they continued with their usual hunting routes in the small forest, not yet daring to cross the Edge. Luckily enough, after a couple of days of not finding so much as mouse droppings, they stumbled upon a stag that had wandered into their section of the forest, undoubtedly coming from the Edge that they took down and brought home.

At dinner that night, they were sure to clue in Ogden, Seamus, Wallais and Beatrice in on their plans, as well as what they ran into when Lance and Shushannah had gone to what they were now calling: the Wild, describing to them the Tested they encountered.

"There's other people out there," Seamus asked, his eyes wide.

"Yes," Shushannah said, "But they aren't people you would expect. They stalked us through the Wild and ambushed us."

"How did you two make it home then?" Ogden questioned, his voice nearly a whisper.

"A girl saved us. Her name is Rosalie. She helped us to find a safe place to spend the night.," Lance interjected.

The pair gave a recount of their night in the Wild. Describing the house they stayed in and what they saw. Despite hearing about the Tested, Wallais and his family were excited about the presence of animals in the Wild. They kept the conversation short, ending abruptly once some Outsiders began to leave the cafeteria.

It had been one full week after Lance and Shushannah had returned to the Community from the Wild, and on the day of the first snowfall of Winter, when the Elders finally called a meeting for the Community.

The four of them stood huddled together, shuddering against the freezing wind in their heavy leather and fur garments in half a foot of snow while they impatiently waited for the Elders to come out and speak. Some Outsiders had started a bonfire, though it was not providing much heat where Lance and his family were standing, and there were too many people for them to squeeze in closer. To nobody's surprise, there were no Founders to be seen outside as they were all staying within the heated hallways of the Alabaster Rampart. Lance watched steam rise from his mouth in thick plumes to entertain himself, though it didn't make him feel any warmer. His face stung from the wind and his nose was numb and running like a sieve.

He stopped playing with the cold air when he saw the Elders finally step out onto their perfectly cleared platform. They were dressed in heavy robes lined with furs, looking very comfortable and warm. Lance was jealous. Elder Sampson was the only one to approach the railing while the other two stayed behind buried under their hoods.

As always, Elder Sampson cast out his hands to bring attention to himself before speaking, though it was not needed as everyone was already looking up at him, wanting him to get the meeting over with so they could go home and warm up.

"Good morning all! I promise not to keep everyone in the cold longer than necessary."

A few murmurs could be heard from the crowd, complaining about the weather, and hoping that the Elders had some good news for a change.

"As per our discretion, a couple weeks ago, we sent two of our best hunters out past the Edge in search of food."

Shushannah and Lance snorted in unison. *Best hunters*, such bullshit.

"I am aware that in the past we have advised you all of the danger that lies beyond our forest's edge, but as the food crisis has reached a dangerous point, we felt it was necessary to determine what these dangers were should food be available. Unfortunately, when our hunters returned, they disclosed that there was no food and no sign of any life to be found beyond the borders of our woods."

Shushannah was red in the face with a throbbing vein in her right temple. Deep puffs of steam rose from her nostrils. They were planning to just sweep the Tested under the rug. "Unbelievable," she whispered, "Un-fucking-believable."

"Are you surprised?" Lance whispered back, "What do you think people here would do if they knew there were other people living out there? There would surely be a revolt. They've been harping for decades that we're the last surviving people on the planet. This is the worst time for them to be proven wrong."

They stopped talking as Sampson resumed his speech.

"As this is the case, we will no longer pursue anything beyond the confines of the forest surrounding our Community. This unfortunately leads into the next topic of our meeting this morning. We have all spoken in great length to determine a solution for the food issue. The only solution that we believe will be successful is one that you will all be upset to hear. I tell you this so that you may all prepare, but before we explain our solution, we ask that you please keep in mind that we will also be partaking with you in this plan as the only way we will make this work is if we work *together*."

The crowd began to murmur in concern while others began to grow irritated. Lance's stomach fell, knowing that things were about to get a lot worse.

"The solution that we have decided upon is what was called a "culling" in the Old World. This was the act of thinning out the population of a particular animal species that had negatively impacted the ecosystem. At this moment in time, *we* are the species negatively impacting our ecosystem."

The crowd broke into a boisterous roar, directing insults to the Elders, specifically at Sampson. He raised his hands in a feeble attempt to calm the people down. They had all but forgotten about the cold and were now fueled by a hunger and panic induced rage and did not obey Sampson's commands. He was visibly nervous, which told Lance that he was beginning to lose control of the crowd, something that had never happened before.

Sampson was finally able to quiet the crowd down long enough for him to continue his speech.

"Please people, you need to calm down. I understand your rage, but getting angry is not going to fix the situation. What I am proposing is this: we forgo food for a designated period of time and allow our numbers to fall to a more manageable size. In the last few years, our population has grown exponentially to the point that we don't have room within our gates for additional houses to be built. As I said before, myself, Borris and Maxwell will be participating in this 'culling' with you all. There will be no need for violence as we will ration what we have left of the stew in an attempt to keep some food in our bellies. It will be a tough process, but one that will help our Community in the long run. Once our numbers have reduced to a more manageable count, we will enact new rules to assist us in the future from avoiding an incident like this happening again. I assure you all, this was a measure that we did not wish to take, but one that is crucial for our survival. I ask that you all be patient as we go through this process. I thank you for joining me, you may all return home to spend time with your families to avoid being out in this cold more than is necessary."

"How can you say that when all of you 'Founders' are sitting inside a heated room while we all freeze our asses off? How are we supposed to know that we aren't being starved out while you all fill your gullets behind our backs?" a man yelled from the crowd. A chorus of voices demanded an answer from Sampson.

"Please people," he began again, his confidence again wavering, "We can't afford to turn on one another now. These titles have come up again and again, splitting us up as a whole, but we cannot let this happen! If we are going to get through this, we need to get through this together and not by fighting with one another. In order for us all to get through these trying times, we need to trust one another."

"That's a load of shit," the same man yelled again. Lance tried to figure out if it was someone he knew or not. "You all sit up there on your high-horses! It's easy to tell us to trust one another when you live in luxury while we live in the mud and filth, hoping we don't freeze to death at night! Now on top of all that, you expect us to just sit around and wait to die?!"

The crowd again erupted in agreement, their rage increasing. Sampson stepped away from the railing, his nerves unwinding more and more.

"I hear what you are all saying," he said with a calm voice, "But again I state, we cannot attack each other! We can discuss issues in a calm manner instead of shouting at one another and causing an uproar. I understand where you are all coming from as our living situations are drastically different from each other, but that doesn't mean we are valued differently. Every single one of you down there is just as important as us. Your lives *all* have meaning. I again urge you all to return home and spend time with your families. Once we have gotten through this, we will discuss how to make all of your needs feel addressed."

Without waiting to hear further from the crowd, the Elders quickly turned their backs and retreated back into the Alabaster Rampart. Outraged cries from the crowd chased them, but soon quieted down once the people realized they would receive no answer.

The crowd dispersed with irritated mutters and a thick tension looming over everyone's heads. Lance and his family trudged back home through the freezing snow, eager to get in front of the fire to warm their frozen flesh. As he made the trek back, he could see the anxious looks on his neighbors' faces knowing that the Community was the closest that it had ever been to its breaking point.

He stomped the snow on boots off once he stepped into the house. Marick brushed the snow back outside once everyone had finished their stomping. Shushannah started a small fire in their little fireplace which everyone huddled around trying to grasp at scraps of heat the tiny flames gave off. Eventually they grew, as did the warmth radiating from the fire allowing everyone to spread out. Lance stopped shaking and changed out of his wet pants and kicked back for a little bit. He lost himself in thought, thinking about what Rosalie was up to with her people. He wondered if she was dealing with a food shortage too—or if she was even still alive. Over the last few days, he found himself thinking of her often, wondering if fleeing the Community with his family was better than staying. It was only a matter of time before tensions overflowed. He didn't want to be around to see what that would bring.

He pulled out the map he drew and looked over the path he and his mother took. He wished that he asked Rosalie how far they could go out into the Wild before they were in Tested territory, but something told him that the Tested were everywhere in the Wild.

After an hour of looking over the map to the point that his eyes burned and the image was ingrained in his brain, he put it off to the side and rubbed his eyes after giving a long and satisfying yawn.

He pulled back his curtain and sat down at the table with Adelade who was scribbling away with the gnub of a purple crayon, one of the last of her collection that Wallais had sneaked out of the Alabaster Rampart. She didn't look up when he popped a quick peck on her cheek. "What are you drawing?" he asked with genuine curiosity. To him it was a mass of scribbles and congealed colors, but to her it could be anything.

"I think it's a flower garden."

"You think? You're the one making it, how do you not know what it is?"

"I just started drawing and this is what I made. I won't know what it is until it's done."

He chuckled to himself.

"Do you ever get scared?" she asked him, dropping her crayon. She was gazing up at him with misty eyes.

He thought for a moment before answering her as he wasn't sure if he should be honest with her or not. He put an arm around her and answered her honestly. "Yes. I get scared all the time. I was scared when Mom and I were stuck in the Wild. I get scared when I come home from hunting and I don't have food for the Community. But most of all, I get scared when I think of losing you, and Mom, and Dad."

"I was scared when you and Mom didn't come home too. I thought you two had died and I would never see you again."

"I'll always come back. Mom will always come back too. I promise you that. No one thing or one person will keep us from getting back home to you and Dad, okay? No matter how scared I get, getting home to you helps me get through anything."

"Okay," she accepted, but there was a tone in her voice that he could pick up on that she knew he couldn't keep that promise. He knew it himself that if he and Shushannah were out in the woods, outnumbered, they would surely be killed. She resumed her coloring, though the vigor was gone that she had before their conversation.

"You know, it isn't bad to be scared," he continued.

She dropped her crayon again and looked up at him with a furrowed brow. "It isn't?"

"No, not at all. Everybody gets scared now and again. It's a normal thing to feel—especially with everything going on."

"Even Mom gets scared," she whispered.

"Even Mom," he whispered back with a wink.

Her mouth was agape for a moment, disbelief settling in. He smiled and hugged her tightly against him, which she returned wrapping her arms around him.

"You have Dad to keep you safe and we'll always make it back. We're going to be smart and safe. Last time was a fluke, but we'll be ready next time we go out there."

"What's a fluke?"

"It's like when something doesn't go how you expect it to."

"It sounds like a bad word," she giggled.

He laughed with her, some tension leaving his body. He knew this would be hard on her, but she would make it through with the rest of them. It's not like they have a choice anyways.

"What are you teaching her?" Shushannah teased with a raised eyebrow, fully hearing their conversation but wanting to keep the good mood flowing, "Are you teaching her bad words?"

"Lance taught me what 'fluke' means!"

Shushannah gasped in feigned surprise.

"That's a naughty word!"

"No, Mom! It means something didn't go how it should have, like that time you tried to grow flowers outside!"

Lance's jaw dropped and a bellowing laugh escaped his mouth.

Shushannah came over and grabbed Adelade in a hug, kissing her multiple times on the cheek after jokingly calling her a little brat. Lance sat back and watched the scene unfold before him and silently promised himself to hold onto this memory. He turned to look as Marick joined in the laughter too, coming out from behind his curtain, having just woken up from a nap.

He joined in on the family hug, happiness flooding their bodies as they forgot about the food shortage, the Tested, the strain the Community was feeling and just focused on being in the moment with each other. He hoped that this wouldn't be the last time they were together like this, truly feeling lucky to be alive, but something gnawing away in the back of his mind told him that this would not be the case.

That voice couldn't have been more correct.

9

It had been two weeks since the Elders began the culling and tensions had only increased among the population. The Elders were only allowing everyone a single meal for dinner every other day, but each time they received their helping, it was significantly smaller than the meal before.

Tonight was a dinner night, but when Lance and his family entered the mess hall, the sign from the day before was still posted that read: "no meal tonight" on the sneeze guard. With frowns and empty bellies, Lance and his family departed from the mess hall. As they left the Alabaster Rampart, they were drilled with the usual glares from the Founders, which Lance and his mother were quick to return, but Marick chose to keep his head down and pushed Adelade along.

Lance's stomach had been hurting as it contracted tightly desperately searching for even a scrap of food to break down for sustenance. It gurgled in irritation at him, clawing him up from the inside begging for something other than the warm broth to keep him going—anything at all. Despite this, he still could only think of little Adelade. She had been sluggish as of late, her usual cheerful disposition had been replaced with a more monotone, unenthused little girl. It was tough to see her like that, especially when she was always the one keeping everyone else's spirits up.

It was impossible for him to sleep at night with the noise from his stomach and the empty feeling he constantly felt, his body urging him to fill his stomach which only added to his worries about his friends, family, and the overall Community itself when the culling was over. Would they be able to feed themselves afterwards? What were the Elders planning when this was done? Had they even thought that far in advance? He tossed and turned, his growling stomach barely tuning out the sound of the wind that found its way into their little cabin through the small cracks of its imperfect construction. Another thing to keep him up.

It wouldn't be until the early hours just before dusk that he would finally slip into a fitful sleep, only to wake up to his mother's foot kicking him awake to sneak out to the Wild.

After the Elders had announced the culling, his family had made a very difficult decision to put their plan into action and Lance was still struggling with it. He couldn't help but feel guilty feeding his family while the rest of the people around him starved and watched their own family members suffer.

The plan they had put together was that Lance and Shushannah would find a safe area just past the border to store meat to dry it for their consumption later. They would then bring back just enough meat to keep hidden and enough to keep their bellies full until the culling ended.

On their first day back out in the Wild, they found a shed that was still standing with a somewhat sound structure in an area where they were able to find smaller game that they cleaned and turned into strips of jerky. It was absolutely perfect. Unfortunately, the jerky they had hung a couple days wasn't quite ready yet, but it would be soon. It would need to be rationed and split up, not only with their family, but with Wallais and his family too.

It was easy for them to sneak by the stationed guards to go out into the woods. They weren't very bright and didn't pay attention all that well, though Lance figured it had to do with the lack of food sapping their energy. They debated on striking a deal with some of the night guards but thought better of it because all it would take is one slip up for their plan to go asunder and they couldn't afford to let that happen. Instead, they snuck out in the early hours of the morning, scaling the fences during the lapse in time in the guards' patrol route. It took Lance and his mother longer than expected to memorize the patrol routes the guards took, but they eventually mastered them.

After covering their footprints left behind in the snow, Lance hurried to catch up with his mother to find their stash of jerky first before continuing on their daily hunt. It was warmer than usual, but still cold enough to chill Lance to the bone.

"I hope it's ready today," Lance grumbled, holding his gurgling stomach.

"It should be," Shushannah answered with a hint of excitement in her voice.

At this point he didn't care if the meat was ready or not, he was going to eat some. He didn't care if it made him sick. It would be worth it just to have *something* in his stomach.

"Good. I'm surprised we never made jerky before. It seems like it would have been a much more efficient way to store the meat."

"We weren't worried about saving our food before. It all went into the stew where it would eventually just break down into the broth. Now we need the meat to survive."

His mother's words sent Lance's mind back to a happier time when the perpetual stew Gordin served was actually a stew with full pieces of fresh vegetables, flavorful beef broth, squares of meat cooked just right that they fell apart when you pushed them against the roof of your mouth with your tongue—the strings of meat separating and releasing the broth trapped within. He hoped that one day he could have a stew that tasted as good as that. In the meantime, he would settle for the pieces of jerky that they strung up. It had been too long since he had something solid to eat.

Shushannah's snapping fingers brought him back to Earth. "Get your head out of the clouds, you're louder than Ogden on Thanksgiving. You're going to scare everything away within a mile of us," she hissed.

He corrected his footsteps and cast his mother an apologetic glance, hoping to not annoy her any further. He kept his thoughts focused on the task at hand instead of fantasizing about food. It wasn't helping him anyways as it only made him feel hungrier.

Lance had marked the stash location on their map with a little drumstick with a smiling face. They were close now, as they just passed by the last landmark location which was a jagged diamond cut into the bark of an oak tree.

They walked into the shed, seeing the meat still hanging where they left it.

When the pair first found the shed, it had only a table inside, being stripped clean of any and all tools and machinery. It held up very well over the years, the windows were all intact, the roof all in one piece—though it needed a little airing out as it smelled of stale air inside. They were able to put together make-shift food racks with tree branches that were secured to the still-sturdy frame of the shed's interior. After they threw the table out, the shed could fit maybe five people at once. It was rather large, for a shed but much smaller than Lance's house.

Shushannah took one of the two dozen or so strips into her hands, looking it over, feeling it, sniffing it, then turning to Lance with a grin. "They're ready," she said, taking a large bite of the meat with a satisfied grin. He ran over, pulling a piece from the branch greedily and stuffing it into his mouth. He pulled another one down before swallowing the tough ball of meat in his mouth.

"Easy," she warned, we need to feed the others too. No more after that piece. We hunt, make more, and eventually, we can eat our fill. Just a little longer."

He ate the next piece of jerky slower this time, savoring the taste. He watched his mother wrap the pieces up and place them in her bag for safekeeping. Once she was done, she shouldered her bag first before picking up her quiver and bow. Lance had taken a seat on the table outside while he waited for his mother and hopped down once she was ready to go. For the first time in a long time, he was excited again to go out hunting, despite that it meant having to kill animals. The silver lining was that they were going for smaller game and didn't need as much since the mouths they were feeding were exponentially less. The only thing he wished was that the trees were in bloom, the insects were active, and the birds were singing. The dense snow created a soundproofing that only magnified the silence around him.

They hunted well into the mid-afternoon when they took their spoils back to the shed. Lance counted a total of four squirrels and three unlucky rabbits. He waited inside while Shushannah cleaned the animals behind the shed, throwing the inedible livers far into the woods and away from their hiding place. He hated watching that part. If there was anything worse than killing the animals it was cleaning them afterwards.

She then cut the meat into strips and cooked them over a small campfire a distance from the shed that she then covered up with the snow before returning. The cooked meat was then strung up by both of them as the sun began to set.

They trudged back to the Community, both of their spirits high for the first time in a long time.

"Tonight I want to bring some of this to Wallais and his family," Lance stated.

"I think we can manage that. We have a lot more meat drying and I think we can make due the next few days. I think we let the meat dry a little too long."

They reached the fence surrounding the Community, with Lance again covering their footprints in the snow with a broom they stashed in a hollowed out tree stump before the next patrol came by. Lance was happy to see that the snow was beginning to melt in places. It would make sneaking around much easier to do when they didn't have to cover every footprint they left behind. It was beginning to annoy him.

Lance was happy to rush into the warm cabin and strip off his wet clothes. Shushannah was quick to share the jerky with both Marick and

Adelade. They each received two pieces, which they gobbled down the same way Lance had that morning. Adeladc went looking for more but Shushannah stopped her. "No, no. We have to ration this out. I know you're hungry, but we need to share with Beatrice and the others, okay?"

"Okay," she repeated, defeat ripe in her voice.

"Would you want to go see her tonight?" Shushannah offered as a consolation prize.

Adelade's face immediately lit up. "Yes!"

"Alright then," Shushannah said, turning to Lance and Marick, "Let me get changed and we'll head up there, okay?"

The boys nodded in agreement while Lance pulled on a pair of dry pants. He was already preparing his shoulder for the beat down it would receive from Ogden when he walked into their dormitory.

Before they left, they were sure to safely stash the jerky on themselves so that nobody would suspect anything. Once they were done, Shushannah pulled Adelade off to the side. She put on her little jacket on and spoke to her with a serious tone. "Adelade, I need you to do me a favor, okay?"

"What is it, Mom?"

"You need to keep the meat we're bringing to Beatrice and her family a secret, okay? If other people found out about this, we could get into a lot of trouble. So I need you to keep this from the kids at school when you go tomorrow no matter what they say or do. Do you promise?"

"I do. I remember what we talked about before," she said with a smile.

"Good," Shushannah replied, giving Adelade a quick peck on the forehead before standing up.

They rushed through the cold night air, plumes of steam rising from their mouths as they puffed along in a hurry to get to the warmth of the Alabaster Rampart. They stomped their boots off in the atrium, leaving the clumps on the tile floor and receiving disapproving stares from the Founders passing by that watched them dirty up their clean floor. Shushannah smirked with a wave at them, causing them to scoff in disgust before sauntering off. Lance stifled a laugh of his own. He had to admit, it was fun pissing off the Founders.

"Just keep adding fuel to the fire," Marick murmured.

"It helps pass the time," she jabbed back.

They went up to the familiar door they had visited so many times before. Marick rapped on the door lightly with his knuckles. They heard heavy footsteps approaching and the door opened to reveal the hulking mass that was Ogden, complete with his trademark smile.

"Well look who it is," he bellowed making Adelade jump, "Come on in guys!"

They filed in one after the other with Lance in the rear. Ogden smirked and clapped Lance on the back. "Hey, Little One. I saw you hiding back there."

"Hi, Ogden."

He smiled, entering the little home rubbing his sore shoulder. He waved to Seamus and Beatrice who were lounging on the couch. Wallais and Lance did their usual quick embrace before taking a seat.

"So what brings you all here tonight?" Beatrice asked cheerfully.

"Well, we come bearing gifts," Shushannah answered, withdrawing the jerky and placing it on the coffee table.

"Where did you find that?" Ogden asked. He picked up the jerky, looking it over before putting it back down.

"Lance and I have been out hunting. We've been sneaking out to get this stuff. We brought this for you guys so that you can get through this too."

Ogden and Beatrice exchanged a look before she spoke.

"Shushannah, you should keep this for your family. We won't be needing it."

Confusion set in with Lance and his family. It was their turn to share looks of concern.

"What do you mean?" Lance questioned first.

Ogden sighed before answering, his face unnaturally drooping. "The Elders have been lying to the people living outside. They have been feeding us every day for the last week. Jasper has been going out beyond the Edge and bringing back meat for us. We've been trying to get out of the Rampart to sneak some food out, but they have us on lockdown since Seamus and I refused to go out for them when they asked. I'm actually surprised that you were able to get in here without being stopped. They've had guards stationed around the Rampart all week trying to keep people from getting in or out."

"We didn't see anyone," Marick remarked, "Maybe they were put on patrol outside?"

Ogden shook his head "More like stuffing their faces. You can't have an army with empty stomachs."

"I knew those slimy bastards were up to something," Shushannah spat, "I fucking knew they would pull something like this. They've always been against us Outsiders."

"We need to work together," Lance mimicked in irritation and shook his head, "I knew it was bullshit."

"When does he go out?" Shushannah commanded, ignoring Lance, hatred burning in her eyes.

Ogden simply shrugged. "I have no idea. I just know that we get dinner every night despite refusing to go hunt."

"He could be out there with us," she thought aloud.

The notion momentarily made Lance nervous, but the feeling dissipated quickly when he realized that they were *both* sneaking around. It would surely be the final breaking point for both sides of the Community if this information got out. He just hoped that he and his mother wouldn't be strung up in secrecy should the Elders learn of their secret hunts.

"Shit," he whispered.

"You said it," Wallais whispered back.

"Is there anything we can do?" Lance asked the room.

There was no answer from anyone as they all knew that no matter what they did, the outcome would be the same and it would achieve nothing except a permanent fissure in the Community.

For the rest of the evening nothing else was said about the culling or the secret hunting as the two families instead chatted about mundane topics though the heavy anxious feeling hanging overhead the entire time with nobody daring to acknowledge it. Shushannah had packed up the jerky and stowed it away out of sight. Eventually, Lance and his family left Wallais's family's living quarters, then the Alabaster Rampart, and came home to a cold, dark cabin. Shushannah stashed the meat underneath a cupboard in the far corner of the room. They sat together, mostly silent while Adelade slowly colored a picture, though Lance could tell that she wasn't really in the mood to color.

He was the first to turn in for the night. He didn't wish to sit in the tense silence any longer and just wanted an excuse to be off on his own for a bit—to be alone with his thoughts. He kept thinking over and over again about what Ogden had said. He eventually realized that soon the Outsiders would realize they were being duped when nobody would be being buried from inside of the Alabaster Rampart while their numbers dwindled away to nothing. When that happened what would the Elders do next? He remained quiet as the week continued on, brooding over the future of the Community as he and Shushannah stashed more jerky, hunted for more meet, and made sure Marick and Adelade were fed.

The first of the Outsiders was buried at the start of the following week. It was a middle-aged woman that Lance wasn't familiar with. He watched the burial from afar, preferring not to be amidst the depressing ambiance. It was tough enough knowing that he and his family were hiding food from these people, never mind that he could have prevented her death by just sharing a morsel of their stash. In a way, he felt that her death was his fault.

The rationing was more and more distant as time continued to pass. More Outsiders were buried, sometimes multiple people a day. It went from every other day to every two days, and then every three days. The ground was too frozen soon enough to bury those that passed away, so one of the homes left abandoned by one of the dead was repurposed as a makeshift morgue until the ground was soft enough to dig the graves.

The Community was silent, more silent than Lance had ever seen before. Even in the Winter of previous years, people were always out and about, chatting, yelling, just living their lives, but now hardly anyone would be seen outside unless there was a funeral taking place.

After a month, meals stopped being served altogether, starting the final, and longest phase, of the culling. The agitation of the Outsiders began to grow as did their craving for food. Whispers began as they noticed that no Founders had been brought out to be buried as there were already multiple funerals a day for Outsiders succumbing to starvation. The Elders remained silent despite vocal outrage expressed by the Outsiders who were now gathering in a large group outside of the Alabaster Rampart around the clock. Nobody was allowed inside as guards were placed at the front entrance actively refusing to allow anyone in or out of the structure. The only silver lining was that it made it easier for Lance and Shushannah to sneak out to continue providing for their family with the distraction. They kept their heads down staying invisible to both Outsiders and Founders alike.

The Community's luck seemed to only be getting worse as a heavy snow storm tore through their area, covering every surface with snow at least a foot deep that was a chore to wade through. Lance and Shushannah had avoided going out after the storm hit for a while, hoping that the snow would melt before another storm passed through. They watched the days pass by through the window of their cabin, watching more bodies be added to the house at the edge of the compound. It seemed that with every body added to the morgue, another body gathered at the front door of the Alabaster Rampart. The protest was strong, ignoring the snow and shouting to the Elders, begging them to end the culling and begging for answers to questions that everyone already knew the answer to. The Founders and the Elders weren't even trying to hide the fact that they had abandoned the Outsiders at this point.

These gatherings carried on for three days straight, dusk to dawn, until someone in the crowd finally had enough.

It was the middle of the night when Lance was jolted awake by people shouting in a panic as they ran past the cabin. Sleep intoxication still gripping his brain, he stumbled over to the window and wiped away the thin layer of fog that covered the glass pane. He squinted, trying to see what was happening. He was so focused on what was going on outside that he hadn't heard his parents creep up behind him. His father's hand made him jump out of his skin.

"Sorry," Marick whispered, "What's going on out there?"

"I don't know," Lance answered him, "I can't see. I'm going to go outside for a better look."

"No. Stay here. I'll go," his mother ordered. She was already pulling her boots on. He didn't argue with her, as his curiosity didn't outweigh his want to stay inside where it was warm and safe. They watched her force her way out into the snow, her shadow passing by the window as she headed towards the Alabaster Rampart where the commotion was coming from. He had the sudden feeling that he should have followed his mother. He made a silent promise to himself that if she wasn't back in five minutes that he would go out himself, armed, to bring her back.

She came back in three minutes.

She was covered in snow and panting. She was worried and rushing around, grabbing her hunting gear.

"We need to move. Now," she panted.

"Wha—why?" Marick asked watching her dart back and forth grabbing various items and stuffing them into her bag.

"The guards are fighting with the people gathered at the door to the Alabaster Rampart. It looks like they killed someone, but I couldn't tell who. It looks like all out war is starting out there."

"We can't just leave! Where are we going to go? It's the middle of the night in the middle of Winter," Marick cried.

"Lance and I have a place we can take you and Addie to in the woods. We'll be safe there."

Lance began to follow his mother's lead and then promptly stopped. "No," he said, "We can't go. What about Wallais? What about Ogden and Beatrice? Seamus? We can't leave them. What if something happens?"

"What do you suggest?" Shushannah barked, "You think they're going to just let us inside? Why don't you go over and ask them politely? Maybe they'll let you in after they beat you into a goddamned pulp! They're keeping people out because they're leaving us out here to die. They're safe in there because they're Founders. Even though Ogden and Seamus refused to hunt for The Elders they're being taken care of. We need to think of ourselves right now. We need to think of Adelade right now. We can always come back for them later."

Adelade shuffled over, rubbing her eyes with her hair a gnarled and knotted mess. "What's going on?" she mumbled.

Marick scooped her up into his arms with a groan. "We may need to leave, honey," he cooed.

"Why?"

"It isn't safe for us here anymore, sweetie, but don't worry, we're going to take you someplace safe, okay," Shushannah answered for him.

"Oh, okay." She laid her head on Marick's shoulder and was asleep again seconds later.

Lance shook his head in irritation.

"I'm not going. You think we can get through the woods in the dark in snow up to our hips? Don't you think the guards will see a light rushing through the trees and tell someone or follow our footprints right to the shed? What then?!" Lance's voice was rising the more irate he became. "You're going to get us killed going out there right now!"

Shushannah dropped her bag and charged up to Lance, shoving a finger less than an inch from his nose. "This is not up for debate! I am not sitting around waiting for them to come in here and fucking kill us off!"

"I'd rather take my chances that they won't and that they'll break up the fighting instead of freezing to death out there, or condemning us to death when they follow our footprints right up to us! That is if we can even find the fucking shed on all this shit!"

Marick had set Adelade down back in her bed and pushed his way into between Shushannah and Lance. "You two need to stop. Now. We can't afford to have you two at odds with each other."

"We need to leave," Shushannah said again, ignoring Marick.

"No," Lance roared, "You're going to get us—"

He didn't finish the sentence. Instead, it was interrupted by a flourish of orange light. It pulled the trio's attention from each other and over to the window. They could see through the little pane of glass that their neighbor's house had erupted in a roaring flame.

"Shit! Do you see why we need to leave?" Shushannah pushed again.

Lance threw up his hands and stormed off. "Fine! Let's fucking go then. Let's go get lost in the snow! Let's go live the rest of our lives in a four by four fucking room!" He shoved a bunch of clothes into a bag, grabbed his quiver, his bow, and shoved his feet into his boots. "Let's fucking go!" He was seeing red and flung open the door, ignoring the cold air stinging his skin.

He hadn't noticed as the blood was rushing through his ears, but he could hear them now. There was shouting coming from inside of the house now completely engulfed by flames. The people were still inside crying out for help. A crowd had gathered, around the house and blocking Lance's path, throwing snow to try and douse the flames but to no avail. His mouth hung open as he watched in horror as the roof of the little house collapsed, sending a flume of sparks upwards into the sky, condemning the people inside to their fate. The fighting at the Rampart seemed to have moved over to the house, as he realized both the guards and Outsiders were throwing snow together to try and smother the flames. They eventually stopped once they finally realized their efforts were futile as the residents of the house had already succumbed to the fire.

His parents stood on either side of him speechless.

He looked at his mother as the realization finally set in.

"Maybe we should go after all," he muttered, "But I'm not leaving without Wallais and his family."

"You're right," his mother finally agreed, "I don't think it's safe for anyone here. We'll get them and then we're out of here."

10

After tensions deflated, the family had a calm discussion about what to do, deciding that it was safest to leave in the morning, especially with the extra guards patrolling around the village once the fire was eventually put out. Only Adelade was able to sleep through the rest of the night while the others refused to move away from the windows, watching the still night air in tense silence.

When morning finally came, the Outsiders were able to fully assess the damage done to the home that went ablaze the night before. The house was completely lost except for the four charred pillars that still stood, standing out against the white blanket of snow surrounding the ruins. The braver of the Outsiders combed through the ashes to find three bodies within the dwelling belonging to the clothier, who as of late didn't have much work to do as the animal pelts he normally worked with hadn't been coming in. It was determined that the fire had started from within the home when the fire the family had made in their fireplace grew out of control after one of the logs sputtered embers onto their hardwood floor while they were asleep. By the time they noticed something wrong the fire had already surrounded them.

Their remains were pulled out and carefully wrapped up so that they could be properly buried.

Their funeral wasn't for another three days when the snow had melted away enough and revealed mud pockets soft enough for the tip of a shovel to pierce. In that time, no more protests took place and no more fights broke out, but Lance could still feel the tension lingering. The leather worker's family were carefully buried after a short funeral. Not many people went as most were hiding inside where it was warm and trying to conserve their energy so as not to join the increasing number of the dead. As the presence of the guards was much heavier, Lance and his family were unable to sneak into the Rampart to get Wallais's family out, so they instead attended the ceremony for the leather worker's family, while also patiently waiting for the right moment to flee from the compound. Lance had spoken with the leather worker on multiple occasions when he commissioned him for some jackets and his boot knife's sleeve when he came of age to have such a tool at his disposal. He was a good man and didn't deserve to die that way and he felt that it was only right for him and his mother to attend the funeral.

The funeral was only a temporary distraction though, and shortly after it was over, Outsiders had once again gathered at the doors to the Alabaster Rampart, blocked now by a wall of guards from going in. They continued to shout, raging louder now with added frustrations from the night of the fire.

To Lance's surprise, the people's cries of outrage were answered.

Elder Sampson came out of the Alabaster Rampart in his heavy, fur-lined robes, backed by Elder Borris and Elder Maxwell as always. The Outsiders quieted down, watching the man glide across the platform to the railing. He looked down upon them, radiating confidence, having visibly recovered from the last speech he gave.

Lance and his family all poked their heads through the windows of the cabin, craning their necks to get a better view of Sampson while still trying to stay inside where it was warm.

"I want to begin with an apology for our silence. I understand the stress that you have all endured these past few weeks while having to bury your friends, family members, and partners, in addition to the terrible events that occurred three nights ago when we lost one of our most valued members of our Community. I stand here today before you all to answer your questions and to try and restore trust to bring our Community together in this trying time."

The crowd stood in stunned silence.

"First and foremost, I want to address your main concerns about what we have been doing with our dead within the walls of the Alabaster Rampart. Those that have unfortunately passed on as a result of the culling have been given proper memorial services and have been put into the incinerator so that we would not need to bury them. Their ashes have been properly placed with their loved ones, and those without, will receive a proper burial come the Spring, as you all are planning to do with those that have passed away outside of the walls of the Rampart. I assure you all, we are dealing with loss inside, just as you all are dealing with it out here."

Lance scoffed. He was lying through his teeth to try and calm people down. Did he take them all for mindless lemmings? "Unbelievable," he whispered. He felt Shushannah nudge him and give a sharp shushing sound as she tried to hear more from her little corner. He puffed air through his nose in irritation.

"If that's true," a woman yelled from the back of the crowd, "Then why haven't we seen the smoke coming from the chimney? It's freezing out here! We would have seen it! What's *really* going on in there? Why are you lying to us?"

A dull murmur broke out in the crowd as the realization settled in. Lance grinned knowing that Sampson was surely getting nervous again.

"The incinerator runs at night as it makes more fiscal sense to run it once a day at the end of the day to conserve our fuel. You wouldn't see the smoke in the dark." It was believable enough, but still an obvious lie. Sampson was clearly just biding his time until more of the Outsiders starved to death—maybe all of them. What was the endgame plan here? How long did Sampson think he could keep up this charade? It was already coming undone in front of him, and yet, here he stood in front of the entire Community and was lying to their faces. That is, unless something changed in between the time Lance last saw Wallais and his family until now, but he highly doubted it.

He tuned himself back into the world as Sampson resumed his speech.

"People, please," Sampson said with more conviction in his voice this time, "We need to remain calm. It is only for a little longer that we will need to continue with the culling before we will again be at more manageable numbers and will be able to hunt for food again."

The crowd erupted in an outburst of anger. They began to shout all at once which made it tough for Lance to decipher any one voice to see what was being said, but he didn't need to in order to know what was causing it, and there was no way of calming these people down unless proof was given—and quickly. Sampson took a step back from the railing in which he had braced himself against. He opened and closed his mouth, much like a fish gasping for air when pulled from the water. He was visibly perturbed and the crowd could sense it.

When it happened, it was so sudden that Lance didn't even know how to fully process it.

It took the crowd a moment to understand what happened too, but when they did, the cries of anger roared louder as one and they pushed forward, brawling with the guards at the doors to the Alabaster Rampart.

As Elder Sampson stepped forward to continue addressing the people of the Community, there was a quick motion of something shooting through the air before it stopped, jutting out from Sampson's left eye. His head shot backward, and as if it were stuck in an elastic band, it recoiled forwards and stopped, a trail of blood trickling down his face from where Lance could see a wooden arrow had pierced through. His mouth hung open as he stumbled backward, falling down presumably dead.

"Oh fuck," Lance exclaimed stepping away from the window.

"Where did that come from? Lance, did you see?" Shushannah asked. She was peering through the windows, trying to see if she could spot the shooter.

"I-I don't know. I think it came from back there." He was pointing towards the back of the Community grounds. He couldn't see anyone, but there were plenty of vantage points for someone to set up to take their shot. But who else had a bow here? Only hunters were allowed, but he supposed that anyone could have made their own, but to shoot from that far away was a shot that only a skilled hunter could have made.

"Marick, get Adelade back from the windows. Stay down and out of sight."

Lance and Shushannah peered carefully through their windows trying to see what was happening outside. The two other Elders had naturally retreated back into the Alabaster Rampart and were hiding in their chambers no doubt. Some of the guards had rushed to Sampson's aid but there was no saving him. The arrow would have without a doubt pierced his brain and any attempt to revive him would be meaningless.

Underneath the platform, Outsiders had clumped together closer to the double doors, violently heaving themselves into the cluster of guards that were doing their best to keep them at bay. It wasn't long before more Outsiders joined the fray, holding various household items. They charged up, spreading the crowd to encircle the guards. The doors remained shut while the guards were pushed into the crowd of twenty or so Outsiders and those not restraining the guards began to bang on the front doors of the Rampart, trying to ineffectively pry them open.

Lance watched and listened as the guards were brutally killed, their cries echoing through the air, just barely audible over the yelling being emitted by the Outsiders. He felt sick to his stomach, wishing he could have gone the rest of his life without hearing the noise.

Shushannah shoved Lance's bow and quiver into his hands. "Get ready," she commanded, brandishing her own bow and arrow. Lance stepped away from the window for a moment to grab his boot knife. His heart hammered in his chest and tendrils of anxiety squirmed in his gut. He stopped for a minute to catch his breath and to get his hands to stop shaking.

"Shit," he heard her whisper.

"What?" he asked looking in the same direction.

His eyes widened when he saw what worried his mother. Founders were spilling out from around the sides of the Alabaster Rampart. They were brandishing weapons of their own and circled around the Outsiders that had now moved on to trying to break down the doors to get inside.

"Where did they come from?" he asked.

"I think from a back entrance. Did you know that there was a back entrance into the Alabaster Rampart?"

Lance shrugged. He couldn't recall there ever being a back entrance that he was aware of over his years of exploring with Wallais, but then again, their exploration was almost always cut short by a grumpy Founder inside telling them that they shouldn't be sneaking around.

"Is it safe in here?" Lance asked his mother, being careful not to say it too loud in case Adelade heard him. She was too busy being comforted by Marick in the back corner to notice much else. He had a worried look on his face, but he was keeping calm despite everything going on.

"I don't know," she whispered back.

He looked at his mother, a woman always confident in her choices, and to see her unsure made him uneasy. He locked his jaw and made sure his quiver was snug on his back and that his boot knife was tightly tucked away.

"I think we should go in to try and get Wallais and his family out," Lance declared, "They could be killed in all this chaos."

"No," his mother stated firmly, "We need to think of *ourselves*. I know it's hard to leave them behind, but we can't risk our lives out there. They can take care of themselves."

Lance shook his head, meeting his mother's gaze. A nervous pit formed in his stomach. "I don't care. I can't leave them behind, especially if we have a chance to get them out before things get worse. One way or the other, I'm going in there. You get Dad and Adelade somewhere safe and I'll come find you after."

"You're not going in there alone," she said, "It would be suicide."

"They would do the same for us, Mom. I know they would."

His mother sighed and was silent for a moment. She looked to Marick and Adelade, then back to Lance.

"We can do this," he told her in a voice much more confident than he felt.

She finally nodded and then looked back to Marick and Adelade. "We'll be back soon. If the fighting makes its way over here and it's too dangerous to stay, get her out of here and we'll find you two. Head for the woods. Take the map and get to the shed. We'll be right behind you."

"You two be careful out there," Marick advised.

With one final glance at each other, both Lance and Shushannah slid through the front door and trotted towards the Alabaster Rampart.

The fighting was clearer now as the Outsiders turned their attention behind them to the Founders that had surprised them only moments ago. Dead from both sides lay on the ground, some bloodier than others. Lance and Shushannah made sure to stay behind the cabins, bobbing and weaving through the compound to avoid being seen by any Founders. They scanned the outside of the massive building, looking for another way in. They kept low to the ground as they made their way to the back of the structure, finding two Founders guarding what they assumed was the entrance. It was a metal door embedded in the ground that looked as if the snow and dirt was freshly wiped away from it. Lance spotted them first and put his hand up to stop her.

"I see two," he whispered.

"Let me see if I can district them," she said, picking up a rock.

She hummed the rock with a popping noise in her shoulder, sending it into a tree on the edge of the compound, but still within earshot of the two guards. They watched as the two guards looked over to the tree, but didn't move. Lance heard his mother huff in annoyance behind him. With the two Founders having their backs turned, Lance motioned to his mother to knock them out. She nodded and pointed to the guard on the right, claiming him as hers to take.

Keeping low to the ground, Lance slunk over behind the guard on the left while Shushannah kept pace with him aligning herself behind the guard on the right. Shushannah pulled the Founder she was behind into a tight headlock while Lance tackled the other to the ground and repeatedly punched him until he was unconscious. They dragged the two Founders off to the side before opening the metal doors and entering a cramped, cement-lined hallway that reeked of mildew. It was just as cold in the hallway as it was outside. It was just wide enough for the pair to walk side-by-side as they felt their way down the darkening hallway.

"Be ready for whatever we find in there," his mother warned, "You need to realize that we may not be able to get out of here without shedding blood. At this point, it is them or us, and I am always going to choose *us* over *them*. When we get inside, you need to have the mentality that these people are trying to kill you and your family. You can't hesitate. Do you understand? Hesitation will get you *killed*."

"Yeah," Lance confirmed with a cracking voice. His throat was dry and scratchy all of a sudden and his tongue felt uncomfortably large in his mouth. He could feel the panic again in his midsection. He tried to focus on getting his friends and family to safety and that he needed to do whatever he had to in order to make it happen. His hands were shaking from the adrenaline pumping through his body.

The hallway seemed to go on forever, but they eventually found the end of it much to his relief as he was beginning to feel claustrophobic. A single metal door painted red blocked what Lance assumed led into the Rampart. Lance dredged up his memories of running around the basement with Wallais as a child, trying to remember if he ever saw this red door before, to know where it would lead them, but he couldn't recall anything.

He watched his mother grab the handle and open the door. Something in his gut told him that there would be people waiting on the other side of the door, that the Founders knew they were trying to infiltrate the Alabaster Rampart. His hands were shaking now, He licked his lips and tasted salt. He was sweating without even realizing it. He wanted to stop her, to tell her that they were about to walk into a trap, but she had already yanked the door open before he could. He let out a sigh of relief to see that it was empty on the other side.

They found themselves standing in a hallway both of them were very familiar with as it was the hallway leading to the kitchens where they would bring Gordin whatever meat they were able to score that day. How had they not noticed this door before? This hallway was always empty, and to Lance's satisfaction, it was empty today as well. He felt a little tension depart from his body, but not much.

He followed his mother to the stairs, looking around his shoulder every other step, paranoid that someone was behind them. He hated feeling like prey. It reminded him of being back in the Wild with those two Tested grunts following them for god knows how long.

They entered the main floor lobby and crept behind a wall of Founders at the windows shouting at the fighting going on outside that were thankfully more interested in what was going on outside rather than what was going on inside, which they took advantage of and ascended the stairs to find Wallais and the others. Lance kept his eyes on the crowd, nearly tripping as he trailed behind his mother wanting to get out of the Rampart as fast as he could.

Upon reaching the third floor landing, Lance could hear sniffling. He furrowed his brow, looking at his mother who shook her head, knowing what he was thinking. He smirked. "I'll catch up with you, let me just make sure it isn't someone that we know."

"Fine," she growled through gritted teeth, "But you get your ass to their dorm soon. We don't have time for this."

They parted ways, Lance going down one end of the hall with Shushannah going the other way. He followed the sound of quiet crying until he stopped at a familiar pair of boots sticking out from behind the door to a storage closet.

"Jasper," he gasped, "What are you doing here?"

"I could ask you the same thing," he sniffed, though the usual discontent in his voice was missing.

He thought for a moment before answering. "I came to check on Wallais with all this shit going on. What are you over here for?"

Jasper wiped his puffy eyes. "I'm hiding. I can't be a part of what's going on anymore."

"*Anymore*? What do you mean by that?"

"My father forced me to go hunting while people outside starved." He was beginning to sob again, his shoulders heaving. "H-he said that I was no son of his if I didn't do it. Do you know how hard it is to say no to him? I just wanted to make him proud of me." The last words came out more of a holler than anything else. Lance couldn't help but pity Jasper despite all the shit he put him through all these years. He knew how it felt to disappoint a parent, especially when you work so hard to gain their approval. "That's why I was always such a prick to you guys, but now I can't do it. I have blood on my hands. I let people die just for my father's approval. I never wanted this to happen. You two didn't deserve all the shit I did to you—you especially."

The pity Lance felt was momentary. He watched Jasper continue to cry without reaching out to him. He felt his own guilt bubbling up, thinking about how he also had blood on his hands by having their own secret stash of food, but he wasn't instrumental in starting an all out war in the Community.

"That's not it though."

Lance furrowed his brow. "What do you mean?"

"My father—he sided with the Tested."

Lance's stomach plunged and his eyes bulged from their sockets. "What? Why? *How*?"

"He went out with me to find them after you and your mom came back. They told him that he could be a leader. They said that if he sided with them we wouldn't starve anymore." Jasper resumed his sobbing.

"How the hell did you guys even find them?"

"They found *us*. We spoke with a small group of them. Some guy named Oscar. Then we met with their leader, Bastion. He told my father that he could lead this place if we joined them."

"What are you telling me all this for?"

Jasper shrugged and shook his head. "I wanted to at least make an attempt to do something good for once. I wanted to try and save at least one person."

"Well it doesn't make up for what you did—not even close."

Jasper's gaze was glued to the floor. He didn't speak anymore and only sobbed quietly. Lance turned on his heel, remembering he needed to meet his mother. He started walking and then stopped a few feet away. He sighed and turned back to face Jasper. He looked pathetic, his legs were spread out now, shoulders slouched and he was breathing through his mouth as his nose was stuffed with mucus from all the crying. He shook his head and turned back heading to Wallais's dorm, moving quickly to catch up with his mother before she tore into him.

He slipped into their room and saw them all packing bags in a wild panic.

"Travel lightly," Ogden commanded the rest. He only had a single bag slung over his shoulder. He was visibly worried and only gave Lance a wave instead of the usual beating on his shoulder. Lance didn't notice as he was still processing his conversation with Jasper.

"About time you got here. Where have you been? Did you find your damsel in distress?" his mother asked with a hint of agitation and sarcasm.

"Yeah, it was Jasper," he answered in a monotone voice, his mind still spinning.

Shushannah raised her eyebrows. "What? *That's* who was crying? What was he all wound up about?"

"He was upset about Outsiders dying, but he had something a lot more distressing than that. He said Maxwell made a deal with the Tested."

Shushannah's face went pale and her eyes widened. "He did *what*?"

Everyone else in the room stopped and stared at Lance. "Maxwell made a pact with the Tested in exchange to be a leader here."

"How could he leave the Community without consent from the other Elders?" Wallais asked.

"He probably didn't," Seamus mumbled, tossing less important things from his bag, "The Elders do things for themselves—especially Maxwell. He's wanted the head Elder position for ages. More than likely he heard the story from Lance and Shushannah about these Tested people and went out with Jasper to talk to them. He's condemned this Community. We're fucked."

The room was silent except for the shuffling of fabric as Beatrice continued to pack the rest of her things. Lance leaned himself up against the wall and rubbed the bridge of his nose. He was thinking his mother's plan to leave was their *only* option of survival, but now it was even more dangerous than before. The Tested knew where they were and now they forfeited that small safety net of space in between the forest around the Community and the Wild. He knew that Outsiders were only a loose end for Maxwell, and with Sampson dead, only Borris remained. There was no place for them here. When the remaining Founders found out what they would have to do in order to survive, many of them would die too. Surely there would be a few that would do what was necessary to survive, to mutilate themselves, just to keep living comfortably in a place with electricity.

After a few more minutes, Wallais and his family stood ready to leave, each with one bag each and the fabrics on their backs. Shushannah stood in front of them, a stern look on her face.

"Stay on our asses. The shit has hit the fan out there. As soon as we get outside, we're going to have to split up. Smaller numbers are easier to hide than a group as big as us. When we're out there, think of these people as animals. They *will* kill you if they see you. You can't hesitate. Ogden, you go with Lance and Wallais. Beatrice and Seamus, you're with me. We'll meet up at our cabin, but if the fighting has spilled back towards it, we'll meet behind the burned house. I need to stop to get Marick and Adelade and then we're getting out of here—*for good*."

Lance had no argument with his mother's plan. He knew that there was no other option at this point. The Community was no longer safe and they had Rosalie to hopefully fall back on once they found her. *If* they found her. They had to get out of here in one piece first.

They silently filed behind Shushannah as they entered the hallway. They went towards the stairs and stopped when they saw Jasper standing and staring out of the window. His puffy face was less than an inch away from the pane of glass. He was still sniffling, but it was apparent that his crying had almost completely stopped. The group walked up to the window and stood beside Jasper.

"They're here," he whispered to Lance.

Lance looked through the glass and saw who "they" were.

Behind the mass of moving bodies was a group of people carrying torches. At the head of the group was a man. He was large, bald, and had two deep scars running down his face. He was clean shaven and smiling. His arms were raised and Lance could see they were heavily scarred as if he burned the flesh. The approach of these men stopped the fighting below. Outsiders and Founders stopped for a moment, perplexed by the new group of thirty or so people standing in a straight line. The bald man was laughing maniacally.

"Who is that?" Lance asked Jasper.

"That's Bastion. He's the leader of the Tested," he answered, "He's the one my father met with."

Lance mouthed the man's name and watched the scene before him unfold.

"Ladies and gentlemen," Bastion began, "May I have your attention please?" The man spoke with a snide confidence that rivaled even that of Jasper on his best days.

Bastion stepped forward. He was wearing tattered orange pants with a rusted looking machete dangling at his side. He had a grungy t-shirt on that had seen better days. He couldn't tell if it was crusted with mud, blood, or both.

"My name is Bastion," he explained, "And I am here to introduce you all to a *whole new world.* I am aware that some of you know you are not the only people left on the planet, while others fail to see the logic foretold by your leaders. I am here now to provide proof to you all that there is life other than your little group on the planet."

The man began to pace back and forth, his hands neatly folded behind his back while he took long, slow strides up and down the line of Tested who were still as statues.

"You see, you are all located in an area that was designated as a red zone, or what we also refer to it as 'uninhabitable', so you will imagine my surprise when I learned that there was a settlement, or a 'Community' as you all seem so keen to call yourselves, smack dab in the middle of the most polluted area in a hundred-mile radius. Of course, I don't know how you can all call yourselves a 'Community' when I walk up and see you butchering each other for who knows what reason, and frankly I don't really give a shit. What I *do* give a shit about is making myself known and giving you all the opportunity of a lifetime and allowing you to join my ranks."

Lance shifted on his feet. He looked over at Jasper who had stopped sniffling and was just about pressed against the glass. The others wore worried expressions on their faces, trying to judge this new threat. Shushannah already knew what to expect from this man, as did Lance, and it was definitely not good. The crowd was even perturbed as both Founders and Outsiders murmured to each other nervously, trying to understand what they were looking at.

Through gritted teeth he continued his speech, "I understand your hesitation. However, I came bearing good—SHUT UP! SHUT THE FUCK UP WHEN I'M TALKING TO YOU!"

The crowd went silent. Lance jumped a little, surprised at Bastion's sudden outburst. His face was red and a vein had bulged from the side of his neck. As the red faded and he calmed down, he adjusted himself and took a breath before continuing.

"I'm sorry. I don't like to lose my cool like that. I just find it rude when someone is talking and people don't pay attention. Anyways, as I was saying, I can save this Community of yours. It was brought to my attention that food is a rare commodity around here. Where I come from, we have fields of it. Yes, actual *fucking fields*. We have meat and grains, more than you had before. Though judging by some of your fat asses, some of you have seen your fair share of food."

The crowd didn't dare make a peep, afraid of upsetting Bastion more as they were not used to someone having an outburst like that. Sampson was always calm about controlling a crowd. This man was a whole new monster.

"I am sure you're all wondering where I obtained this information. Well, I would like to ask that Maxwell please step forward. Maxwell has been instrumental in saving your Community. Maxwell, please come up and bring along your partner, Borris!"

Lance watched as Maxwell bumbled through the crowd, forcing Borris along in front of him. It looked as if Borris had his hands bound behind his back as he was forced up to the front. When they were beside Bastion, Maxwell knocked Borris's legs out from under him, bringing him to his knees.

"Maxwell here cares deeply for this Community and this Community's people. As this is the case, we have made a deal together. If your Community joins my people, we will care for you all as our own. That means, you will be well fed, you'll have roofs over your heads, but more important, we won't burn this place to the ground! The first step though, is to determine one, and only one, leader of this little group here. That one leader then reports to me and advises me of any issues or concerns they may have. So Maxwell, I ask you, please take your place as leader of Community: 1049."

Bastion took the machete clipped to his hip and handed Maxwell, who took the machete with a smirk. Lance's heart hammered in his chest as he watched Maxwell raise the blade over his head with his right arm.

"No, Dad, don't," Jasper cried, fresh tears once again rolling down his cheeks, but his shouts went unnoticed.

Maxwell brought the blade down hard, splitting Borris's scalp down the middle, the tip of the blade sticking out just in between his eyes, stopping just before his nose. Blood sprayed upwards, and the crowd yelled in shock, fear, and anger about what they just witnessed. Maxwell was satisfied—his role of leader finally secured. Bastion placed a hand on Maxwell's right shoulder and smiled as he took the machete back. Lance's mouth hung open, overtaken by disbelief at what lengths Maxwell would go to just to be leader. How did he expect people to follow him now? What trust would they have for him now?

Jasper continued to sob on Lance's left. He looked pitifully at the man that had tormented him his entire life and finally felt for him. He put a hand on his shoulder. Jasper didn't shake it away, but instead looked at Lance from the palms of his wet hands and gave him a small nod as a gesture of thanks.

"Quiet down," Bastion roared, the crowd half-obeying, turning the volume down from yelling to a dull whisper.

"You now have your new leader, Maxwell. Maxwell, I thank you for joining our groups together." He removed his arm from Maxwell's shoulder and turned to the line of Tested that seemed to stand still as statues. He laughed again, and before anyone could react, turned on his heel and brought the machete down quickly, slicing cleanly through Maxwell's neck, cleaving his head completely from his body. The crowd again screamed. Jasper howled in shock to see his father's lifeless, headless, body fall to the ground. Lance slapped a hand over his mouth as Bastion moved, anxious to see what was happening next.

Bastion raised a hand, similar to how Sampson would do to gain the crowd's attention. It worked, as they stood in tense silence staring at him.

"You people now have a choice. You may either join my people or you will be cut down like the filth below my feet have been," he peered around the crowd, eyeing their faces before continuing, "In order to join my people, you must pass a simple test. It is a test of the flesh. Prove to me that the only thing of value is your loyalty to me and you will be fed every night. See the scars on my body—on the bodies of the people standing behind me. We have passed the test. You pass, you live. You refuse, you die."

Nobody in the crowd moved. Everyone inside of the Alabaster Rampart were still in disbelief.

"Fuck this. Kill them all," he commanded, sending forward the Tested who were all too eager to spill blood themselves, "Get the ones in their homes, inside of that big building, all of them! Then, take whatever isn't nailed down! I want this dump leveled by daybreak! I don't want any stragglers to think they can just waltz back home. They don't want to join? Fine! This is how it will be!"

"Mom," Lance started, backing away from the window.

"I know," she answered, "It's time to go."

11

Lance grabbed Jasper by the shoulders and pried him away from the window. "We need to go," he yelled at him as he struggled to get control of Jasper's squirming body.

"No, Dad! Dad," he kept shouting as he tried to run back to the window.

"Leave him," Shushannah barked.

"No! He comes with us!"

"Dude, just leave him. He was nothing but an asshole to us. What do we owe him?" Wallais reasoned.

Lance looked at him with a frown. He stepped up to his friend after letting Jasper go and said, "We don't owe him shit, but just because he's a dick doesn't mean he deserves to die. Look at the people out there. Do you think he deserves the same fate? Do *any* of you think that?!" He turned to look at Ogden, Beatrice, Seamus, and his mother. They didn't protest with him and only looked at him with somber expressions.

"I'll be responsible for him if anything happens. Let's go," he said flatly, guiding Jasper down the hall towards the stairs where they would be making their escape from the Alabaster Rampart. He hoped that he wouldn't regret bringing Jasper later, but he would cross that bridge when he got there, right now he had to get home to his dad and sister before anything happened to them. "You make sure you keep moving. Don't slow us down. Don't make me regret bringing you with us," he murmured to Jasper.

"I won't," Jasper promised. He had started walking with more confidence, but he was still wiping tears from his eyes. Lance could feel his mother's eyes digging into him from behind, but he ignored it for now. He would deal with her later.

They had just made it to the stairs when they heard a crash accompanied by the sound of excited shouting. Lance readied his bow and hunched his body, his senses now running on high alert. They hurried down the stairs, listening to the muffled sounds of people being butchered by the Tested as they tore through the Alabaster Rampart fueled by bloodlust.

They were able to get to the second floor landing before the door from the first floor landing beneath them burst open, followed by the pouring in of a chaotic jumble of Tested, Founders, and Outsiders shouting and fighting with each other. Lance pulled Jasper back by the collar of his shirt and waved everyone back, ushering them back into the hallway to safety. He pushed Jasper behind him, pulling an arrow from his quiver and readying himself while his mother guided the group away. They all backed into the first room they could. Shushannah locked the door and pressed her ear up against it while Lance kept himself at the ready and tried to listen to the noise in the hallway. Lance didn't dare move a muscle, listening to the rapidly thudding footsteps growing closer.

"What are you people doing in here?" a man demanded behind them, making everyone jump out of their skin.

Lance spun to see a family standing against the windows on the far wall. Their furniture was overturned to form a make-shift barricade and the man standing in front was holding a large kitchen knife straight out with both of his hands shaking uncontrollably. A woman and little boy were hiding behind him with tear-streaked faces.

"We aren't going to hurt you," Shushannah said slowly, "You need to be quiet. They're out there and will come in if you don't keep your voice down."

"F-fine, but don't come any closer." He didn't speak any further but he refused to lower the knife.

Shushannah resumed her place at the door while still keeping the man in her peripheral.

"Hey, man. I want to apologize for earlier," Wallais whispered to Lance.

"Don't worry about it, let's just get out of here, yeah? We'll worry about it later."

Lance stole a glance at Jasper over his shoulder. He seemed to be in his own little world again. He sat with his back against the wall and his knees drawn up to his chest. He had his arms wrapped around his shins and was staring straight ahead while muttering something to himself with no expression on his face.

"He looks like shit," Wallais said, looking at Jasper with a pitiful look.

"This doesn't totally change everything between us," Lance warned, "He was still a dick to us growing up but I don't think he deserves to die over that. Maybe this is his chance to try and make it up to us."

"What if he doesn't?"

"Then we cut him loose. We owe him nothing. Trust me, he's not exempt from all this just because he shed a few tears."

"Good," Wallais whispered back.

Lance looked to his mother who was still pressed against the door. He could hear the sound of faint screams mixed with thudding feet. He couldn't pinpoint where exactly they were. If they were going to get out of here they needed to be smart about it. She held up a finger for a moment before giving a thumbs up. She opened the door and the group filed out behind her single-file, leaving behind the very frightened man and his family. Jasper needed minor coaxing, but he followed them all out too. The door was barely shut behind them when Lance heard the door lock click. "Asshole," he muttered before sticking a middle finger up against the peep hole on the door.

He felt naked standing in the hallway. There was nowhere to hide. Nowhere to escape the Tested if they found them. He could hear their maniacal laughing echoing through the halls, mixing with the screams of torment from the unlucky souls that crossed their paths as they cleared out the building. Lance assumed their best way out was through the back entrance as he believed there would be people stationed out front, the only known entrance and exit to the Alabaster Rampart, while the other Tested cleared the structure from top to bottom, with their remaining members waiting outside for those that flee from the massacre inside. It would be designed to leave no living soul left alive so they could take this place for themselves. They were like animals stuck in a corral. Maxwell had led himself and the entire Community to slaughter as a result of his hunger for power.

Community: 1049 would be no more than a distant memory after tonight.

They again moved towards the stairs but stopped short when the body of a woman plummeted down from somewhere up top, landing with a heavy thud on the cement floor of the basement landing. Crazed laughter of two men could be heard as their hurried footsteps clambered down the stairs like children rushing to see what they did.

Lance nocked an arrow against his bow, and aimed it at the empty hallway leading to the stairs. He cleared his mind the best he could and kept his aim steady. His heart hammered in his ears in unison with the Testeds' footsteps inching closer and closer. From his peripheral he could see his mother beside him on his right also aiming in the same direction. "Remember," she whispered, "No hesitation. It's them or us."

His mother's words ignited his panic. He was about to take the life of a human being. His trepidation held fast, causing his muscles to turn to stone for a moment.

It was that moment of hesitation that caused his arrow to miss when the pair of Tested came into view. His mother dropped the man on the right, but the one on the left came running down the hall, tackling Lance to the ground before either himself or his mother could load another arrow. Ogden moved first, plucking the man from Lance easily with his massive paws. In the brief moment they were face to face, Lance could see that the man was missing an eye and had what looked like the bottom of a broken glass bottle shoved in the socket. He had also filed his teeth to points and had heavily scarred lips. He was biting at Lance like a rabid animal, spittle flying from his mouth.

Lance scrambled to his feet just in time to see another trio of Tested bolting down the hallway towards them. An arrow flew past Lance's head on the left side, burying itself deep in the chest of one of the Tested on the left. Seamus tackled the other on the right while Lance charged at the man in the center, who was missing all but one tooth. Lance drew his boot-knife as he ducked from a horizontally swinging fist. He brought the knife up hard right under the man's chin without thinking. He felt sick as he felt his blade puncture through flesh and warm blood poured down his hand. The man fell down dead with the knife still sticking from the bottom of his head.

Lance couldn't blink or pull himself away from the sight. Blood was rushing through his ears and he dry-heaved. A strong hand pulled him as they continued back on their path back to the basement. He was thrown hard against a wall, jarring him from his daze. "Get your shit together," his mother hissed in his face, "Stay focused! We need to get to your father and Adelade!"

Adelade. His father. Yes, he needed to think of them. He needed to get to them.

He forced himself away from the wall and readied another arrow. He felt a bump on his right arm. Wallais had his hand extended, holding Lance's boot-knife out to him. The blade was cleaned. He pushed it back to his friend and shook his head. "Hold on to it for now. I'd rather you have it and not need it, than need it and not have it. It'll make keeping you guys safe a little easier." Wallais nodded and held the handle of the knife tightly as his arm dropped to his side.

Lance didn't really want the knife back anyway, not after what it had just done. What *he* had just done.

They were able to make it to the stairwell without any more surprises. Descending the stairs quickly, sometimes taking two at a time, they reached the basement level where the body of the unlucky woman from before lay unmoving in an awkward position. Lance looked down at her in horror. She had been killed long before her body hit the ground, judging by the knife jutting from the middle of her forehead. Her eyes bulged from their sockets, with a look of pure terror forever cemented on her face. Her limbs were bent in awkward positions after the impact on the cement. He could tell she was a Founder based on her clothing, but if you asked him, he would never be able to pick her face out of a crowd. He forced himself to keep walking, shaking his head, knowing that the whole situation could have been avoided. If Maxwell wasn't so stupid, maybe that woman would have still been alive. Maybe more people in the Community would be alive.

Almost immediately after that thought finished, his throat closed with the realization that the Tested could have gotten into their little cabin by now. They could have Adelade right now.

He picked up speed, keeping in stride with his mother, his mind focused on getting to his sister and his father. He needed to be sure they were safe. He clenched his jaw and his hands balled into fists promising himself that he would do whatever it takes to get to them.

He caught his mother looking at him, concern masked by approval for how he was handling the situation. He was becoming her soldier after all.

They made it to the secret passage door without any other issues much to their relief. They filed through one at a time with Shushannah in the lead and Ogden trailing in the back. Lance couldn't help but feel claustrophobic while going through the hall, wishing that he could get back out into the open as fast as possible. Just before opening the door, Shushannah turned and faced the group.

"Remember the plan from earlier. Jasper, you stick with Lance. If it were up to me, I would have left your ass in there as fodder for those assholes, but for some reason he felt the need to take you with us. You're *his* problem now."

Through the darkness, Lance could see the downhearted look on Jasper's face as he averted his gaze to the floor. If Lance didn't remember all the shit he and Wallais went through growing up, he would feel worse, but he had to admit that Jasper finally getting payback for the years of torture he caused to him and Wallais. Despite that, Lance knew he was a human being and deserved a chance to redeem himself if he was actually telling the truth about wanting to do some good. After seeing the death of his father, Lance thought it best to maybe not be so hard on Jasper for a bit. He put a hand on his shoulder before they walked outside to the grounds of the Community. Now was a time to band together, not to put each other down regardless of the past.

Without speaking another word, Shushannah opened the door and one by one they clambered out into the cold air. Lance happily noticed that the Tested hadn't set up behind the Alabaster Rampart. He figured that the universe needed to stop shitting on them at some point.

Shushannah motioned for the group to split as previously decided, with the new addition of Jasper, standing sheepishly beside Lance. There would be no more speaking from here on out. He grew anxious thinking of all the horrible things that could have happened to his father and sister while he and his mother were gone.

Lance took point as he pushed the thoughts from his mind and focused on getting back home. Jasper trailed directly behind him, followed by Wallais, and Ogden bringing up the rear. They silently stalked through the dense shadows the trees created for them. They could hear the cries of unlucky members of the Community from all around being torn apart by the Tested. Amidst the cries of fear were cries of bloodlust as the Tested satiated their need to kill and conquer. There was a heavy smell of smoke and flickering light from flames as the Tested went through the grounds, burning every structure they could, laughing in hysterics. Some people didn't have a chance to get out in time or were barricaded inside as the sound of their yelling was just audible over the roaring flames. This wasn't even about taking over for the Tested anymore, the people of the Community were just playthings for them to have their way with.

Lance was sure to keep an arrow at the ready, his eyes narrowed and darting around, being sure that they were completely hidden. He occasionally peered back to be sure the others were with him. Their faces were pale, colored this way by the light reflecting off the moon's surface and down to the ground below. He tried to keep an eye out for his mother, hoping that she was staying safe with the others.

They were almost to the cabin now—almost in the clear. He could see it, and to his relief, it was still standing and appeared untouched, but it was only from the back and there was no telling what the front of it looked like. There was no light inside which could either be a good or a bad sign, though he was still trying to stay hopeful that his family was safe inside, hidden away from the nightmare going on around them or long gone and waiting at the shed as planned.

He swallowed down a nervous lump and kept going.

They traveled forwards about another twenty feet before Jasper tripped behind him with a soft grunt. Lance turned to help him up when Jasper pushed him aside and bolted ahead, through two houses to the middle of the grounds. "Fuck," Lance hissed under his breath. He turned back to Wallais and Ogden. "You two keep going. I'm going after him before he gets us all killed. Stick to the trees until you are *absolutely* sure you aren't being followed or walking into a trap."

Ogden put a heavy hand on Lance's shoulder. "I hope you know what you're doing. Your mother would kill me if anything happened to you, Little One," he whispered.

"She would kill me too," Lance joked back, "You get to the cabin and meet up with her. We'll be there, I promise."

Ogden gave a nod of approval, at which time Lance took off after Jasper, keeping an eye out for any Tested that may be skulking around waiting for them. He found Jasper standing still, shoulders slouched and unmoving staring straight ahead. As Lance approached, he saw what exactly had caught Jasper's attention.

Mounted on stakes were the heads of all three Elders. Maxwell was in the middle, his eyes beginning to gray through drooping eyelids, his mouth hanging open lazily. Lance slowly approached Jasper, still being cautious of the area around them. It wouldn't be hard to spot them now, they were in the center of the compound with nothing sheltering them from view.

"Jasper, we need to go," he urged.

He tried to pull Jasper, but he refused to move. His eyes were fixated on his father's head, fat, silent tears rolled down his cheeks. Lance sighed heavily through his nose. He needed to do something and fast.

After a quick thought popped into his head, one that under normal circumstances he wouldn't consider, but he was desperate to get Jasper out of there and to get back home to his family. He reluctantly unshouldered his bag and pulled out a shirt. In disgust, he wrapped it around the severed head of Maxwell and pulled it from the stake with a stomach-churning squelching noise, leaving behind blood on the pointed piece of wood. He wrapped Maxwell's head up and stuffed it into his back, replacing it on his shoulders. "We will bury him properly, but right now we need to go," he whispered.

His actions seemed to have jolted Jasper from his trance and he was looking Lance in the eye, silently thanking him. Lance yanked Jasper away, breaking into a jog and feeling the contents of his bag moving around with every step. He tried not to think about the solid mass bumping into the square of his back. If you told him that morning that he would be stuffing the severed head of Elder Maxwell into his bag, he would have told you that you were absolutely bat-shit crazy, but now look at him. Everything around him was unraveling, but he had to keep going. There were too many people relying on him and he couldn't let this get to him.

They bolted back to the safety of the shadows, being sure that they weren't followed and finally made it to Lance's cabin. He couldn't see anyone else, nor could he hear anything from inside. He put up a hand o Jasper, telling him to wait, while he crept forwards to inspect the house.

He arrived at the back of the cabin and peered into the window. He could see that the front door was ajar, allowing the pale light of the moon to show the overturned interior of the house. The kitchen table was broken and thrown to the side along with a couple of overturned chairs, but he couldn't see anything more than that. A hollow feeling formed in his stomach as thoughts of his sister and father being ripped from their home and butchered by the Tested flooded his mind.

No.

He couldn't think like that.

He couldn't think like that until he was sure.

With heavy, unsteady legs, he hugged the exterior wall of the place he once called home, being sure to move without making a single noise. He came to the front door frame, which was splintered from where a heavily placed foot kicked the door open. He immediately noted a trail of dark liquid coming from behind the drawn curtain where his parents slept. Shards of wood covered the floor from both the door and the destroyed furniture. He entered the cabin, seeing the carnage in full that had been committed. His "room" had been ransacked, his blankets shredded, books ripped apart, and his curtains torn down from the walls. Their wash basin was shattered and a small puddle of water was spread on the wooden floor, just about fully absorbed by the wood or soaked through the cracks to the soil beneath. Everything that he knew and loved lay around him broken into pieces, and all for nothing. All of his memories, the entirety of his life was in this place, and to see it in this condition crushed him, but he had a more immediate concern on his mind.

He quickly crossed over to the curtain and poked his finger into the liquid. It felt sticky and smelled metallic. In the moonlight he could tell that it wasn't black but was red like a wild rose. There was no mistaking that this was blood, but whose blood was it? He wasn't sure if he wanted to know, but he *had* to check. He needed to be sure, but who else could it be?

He grabbed the curtain with his right hand. His mouth was dry and he felt as if all of the air had been pulled out of his lungs. Without any further hesitation, he ripped the curtain aside and took a step back.

At first it was hard to tell who or what he was looking at. He knew it was a person, that much was clear. The body was strung up upside down and stripped naked. They had been completely gutted like a deer, cleaned out from the inside, down to the spine that was peeking out from scraped muscle tissue. Looking down further, he saw that their hands were bound behind their back, slices ran up and down both arms, deep enough that yellowed bone was exposed. His eyes moved further down to the person's face where they lingered in earth-shattering horror.

His father.

It was Marick hanging there, gutted like some wild animal. His entrails were left in a pile on top of the blankets his parents once used to sleep on. Tears pumped from his eyes, vomit erupted from his mouth and he fell backwards onto the floor, shock hitting his system. No noise could escape his mouth as he tried to scream. He couldn't tear his eyes away from his father, no matter how hard he tried. Then it hit him.

Where was Adelade?

He scrambled to his feet, looking around for a sign of his sister. He began to frantically search her things, flipping her own stack of blankets, finding nothing.

"You like the decor," a gravelly voice taunted from behind him, raising the hair on the back of his neck.

Lance turned to see two Tested silhouettes darkening the doorway to the cabin. He was able to raise his bow and arrow, aimed perfectly at the person on the right.

"Put down that little stick shooter, boy." He couldn't tell which person said it.

"Like hell I will," he growled, "First one of you to step forward gets the arrow and I won't fucking miss."

"Did you see what we did? Do you like it? It took us a while."

Lance's eyes darted momentarily to the corpse of his father hanging against the wall. "You two did this," he seethed, rage boiling in his veins.

"Oh yes we did. We had fun with him too. Too bad we didn't get to the little one. She ran off somewhere. Did you know them?"

Lance's vision became hyper-focused as his senses magnified everything around him. Something inside of him had finally snapped and was ready to be unleashed. He wanted to make them pay. He wanted to make them all pay. He felt light-headed as his body surged with a drunken rage.

Without so much as a moment of hesitation, he released the arrow, sending it flying directly into the center of the forehead of the man on the right, killing him instantly. He tossed his bow to the side and charged the man on the left, ducking just in time to avoid a swinging blade. He drove his own cocked fist straight into the man's stomach, forcing him to double over in pain. In one swift motion, Lance grabbed the man's long greasy hair and drove his knee straight into the man's face, hearing a satisfying crunch as blood poured from the man's broken nose. Still holding the man's hair, he yanked him down to the ground, mashing his face into the floorboard. As the man scurried to his feet, he was still grinning through the blood that had stained the front of his face. He waved the machete in his right hand menacingly, taunting Lance. The man laughed gleefully, only feeding into Lance's fury. He was playing with him. As the man charged forward, swinging the machete, Lance side-stepped, grabbing the man's arm and twisting it behind his back. He kicked the man's legs out from under him and, once the man was on his knees, snapped the man's arm backwards at the elbow with his knee.

The man hollered in pain, dropping the machete to the ground. Lance planted his boot into the small of the man's back, forcing him down again and picked up the machete. He wasn't even aware of what he was doing and watched himself move as if he were outside of his own body. An enraged roar belted from his mouth as he repeatedly brought the machete down, cutting into the man's back. He felt wet as blood coated his arms and clung to his hair and face. When he was satisfied that the man was dead, he drove the machete through the back of what remained of the man's head for good measure before tearing it free and stepping over his body.

He stood for a moment on his feet, swaying, drunken with a fury he had never known before, wanting and needing to expel more of it on the Tested. He ripped the arrow from the other man's corpse as he made his way outside after grabbing his bow. He stumbled from the ransacked home and started walking towards the Alabaster Rampart with a white-hot fury driving him. He was looking for Bastion. He was looking for more blood to spill and more revenge to take on these people.

Jasper approached him from his right side but he didn't see him as his rage was blinding him to everything around him except for his destination.

"Don't go that way, they're over there," he whispered trying to pull Lance away.

Lance shook him off without a word, but a pair of strong hands belonging to Ogden pulled him up into the air like a sack of potatoes and hauled him away. He squirmed and struggled but it was no use.

"Hush," Ogden whispered, "We will get vengeance, but not today. Not today, Little One."

Tears fell from Lance's eyes as his anger was left unsatisfied. Eventually exhaustion took over and he no longer had any fight left in him. He just allowed himself to be dragged away from the Community, from his home, and from the body of his father. His body went limp, at which time Ogden adjusted him, passing his bow and quiver to Jasper. Wallais looked on with concern, holding the bloody machete in one hand, but kept silent, not knowing what to say to his friend.

Ogden guided them to the woods, a crumpled piece of map in his left hand while he braced Lance with his right.

Lance was lost in a trance. The vision of his father hanging from the wall was all he could see. He didn't get to say goodbye. He didn't get to show his father what life was like beyond the Edge. He would never laugh with, talk to, or explore with his father again. He was gone. With this realization, tears poured from his eyes. He felt Ogden's surprisingly gentle hand pat his back as he cried, wanting nothing but to see his father again. He wrapped his arms around Ogden and let himself be comforted.

Eventually, they made it to the little shed where Lance and Shushannah had been storing their jerky. Shushannah, Seamus, Beatrice, and Adelade were all waiting inside. When they saw Ogden approaching, they burst from the door.

"What happened?" Shushannah gasped, seeing Lance's condition, which was now zombie-like as he simply stared into space too physically, mentally, and emotionally exhausted to do anything else.

"He saw Marick," Ogden confessed, "I couldn't get to him in time. He was getting ready to head back into the Alabaster Rampart when I grabbed him. He put up a bit of a fight, but he calmed down."

Ogden gently set Lance down on the ground in a seated position. Shushannah knelt down and put a gentle hand to his face. She pulled him in for a tight hug, a hug in which he did not reciprocate. It felt strange to him, even in his comatose state, he was alert enough to note what his mother did. He couldn't remember the last time she hugged him.

"Who's blood is that on him?" she asked.

Ogden looked down at her gravely.

"The Tested. He cut one of them into little pieces with his own machete. Something inside of him broke, Shannah."

She looked at her son who was still unresponsive. He looked past her, the image of his father's body permanently transfixed in his vision.

Adelade came out of the little shed, her eyes red from crying. She saw her brother and immediately went to him. The little girl climbed into Lance's lap and hugged him tightly. She cried softly into his chest. He stared ahead blankly with his arms hanging limply at his sides while his legs stuck out in front of him awkwardly. If he wasn't breathing, he could have easily been mistaken for a corpse. After a little while, he was brought into the shed and laid down on a makeshift bed. His mother cleaned him gingerly while looking at him with concern. After she left, he didn't sleep and instead let the last image of his father he would ever see fester in his mind.

Hours later, his rage began to build again, shaking him from his unresponsive state. It was still dark when he joined the others outside that were still awake. They all looked at him waiting to see what he was going to do or say.

He approached Wallais who was absentmindedly twiddling with Lance's boot knife. He gently took it from his friend who had a confused look on his face. He then returned to the shed where he sat down and rolled up the sleeve on his left arm. He took the knife and cut three deep lines into his arm, deep enough to draw blood and scar, but not deep enough that the skin wouldn't heal. Three lives he had taken.

No, not lives.

Three Tested he killed. He promised himself that he wouldn't be like them. That even though he butchered that man only a few hours ago, that he would retain his humanity. The lines on his arm would not be trophies but instead of a reminder of the people he killed.

He shoved the boot knife into its usual slot on his right boot and laid down in his makeshift bed. His arm stung as the cold air seeped into the fresh cuts, but he ignored it. Before sleep finally took over, he made a silent vow to himself and to his father. He vowed that any time he crossed paths with the Tested, he wouldn't let them get away. He would remember what they did to him and to his people. The Tested scarred themselves to prove themselves, while Lance would scar himself to keep himself human. His mother was right, the Tested aren't people. To Lance, the Tested were parasites that needed to be eradicated from the world.

His father would get the redemption he deserved. He would bring justice down on the Tested no matter what.

12

The following morning Lance forced himself up on shaking legs. He had slept in the far corner of the shed, curled into a ball. He stood up and stretched, his back crackling and a small groan escaping from his mouth. His muscles ached from the day before, his adrenaline now wearing off. His stomach growled but he didn't feel like eating. He was still playing the events from the night before over and over again in his head. The images were burned into the back of his mind. The Elders' heads on stakes, his father used as some sort of sick enjoyment for the Tested, and the burning down of Community: 1049.

His bag was hanging against the wall on a nail. His blood ran cold when he remembered what was in it. He hoped nobody went through it while he was asleep, otherwise they would have had quite a nasty shock.

It looked as if everyone had gone outside already. He scrubbed his hair roughly and stepped outside. He wiped away crumbs of dried blood on his pants. As expected, everyone was gathered together, bickering amongst each other about something. It was obvious that last night hadn't just affected him negatively. He approached, not being noticed as the group was too busy arguing with each other.

"Hi, guys," he said as nonchalantly as he could.

Everyone stopped and turned to look at him. He gave a wave and a half-hearted smile. "What's going on?" he asked with genuine curiosity. Something told him that they were talking about him because o how fast they all stopped.

"How are you feeling?" his mother asked.

He sighed. "Good for someone that saw the dead body of his father hanging from the wall, killed three people and lost the only home he's ever known."

His mother did not smile at this. "I was trying to stop you from seeing that," she said gravely, "I'm sorry, I couldn't get to you time."

Adelade was silently sitting at her side, staring straight ahead with no emotion much like Lance was last night. The realization hit him that she was there to actually *see* what those monsters did to their father, not just to see the aftermath like he did. He knelt down on one knee and tried to take her into his arms, but she gave a cry of protest and clung to their mother's pant leg tighter. "Let her be for now, Lance. Give her some time. She's been through a lot."

He got to his feet, feeling a tightness in his back from the wooden floor. He rolled his neck and began to speak. "I think we should hold funerals for Dad and for Maxwell."

"For Maxwell," his mother barked, "The man that caused all of this shit to happen in the first place?!"

Lance cast a glance towards Jasper before arguing back. He was being smart and keeping his mouth shut, his eyes cast downward at the earth, suddenly finding something very interesting to look at.

"Yes. Yes, I think we should. Jasper deserves to be able to put his father to rest and so do we!"

His mother silently pouted, knowing she would not win this argument with him. She knew deep down that it wasn't about Marick or Maxwell anymore as they weren't around to see this. It was for their children to honor them so that they could properly mourn and move past the events of yesterday. Lance turned and walked back towards the shed.

He grabbed his bag from the hook and slowly made his way over to the group who was staring at him, wondering what he needed his bag for. "Don't go behind the shed, and *especially* keep Addie from behind there," he warned. Shushannah furrowed her brow in complete confusion but didn't speak and instead watched her son. He retreated around to the back of the shed where he opened up his bag and pulled out the bloody fabric containing the head of Maxwell. He gently set it down on the ground.

After shouldering his bag, he went into the shed and emptied his bag in the corner and grabbed his bow and quiver. The group was silent as he approached, looking to see what was going to happen next.

"Behind the shed is all I could get of Maxwell so that Jasper would follow me out of there. I couldn't get anything of Dad, so I don't know what we can bury in his memory."

"I-I have some of his clothes packed," Shushannah advised, "We could bury those."

Tears were pooling in her eyes now. Her shell was crumbling away and he knew she hated that. She hated to show emotion. He remembered the only time he ever saw his mother cry as a child when her father had passed away. He caught her alone behind the cabin crying silently. He went to hug her and instead was pushed away and told to leave. They never spoke about it again.

"Does anyone have a shovel?" he asked aloud.

Everyone shook their heads.

"Just as I thought. I'm going to go collect some rocks to make a burial shrine."

"I'll go with you," Wallais offered.

Lance nodded with a half-hearted smile. He knew he could always count on Wallais. He retrieved his own bag and the two set off into the woods. Jasper didn't speak or make a motion to follow them, which annoyed Lance. Jasper would need to properly carry his own weight from now on if he was going to stick around. Both of them had lost their father last night but yet it was only Lance and Wallais out gathering rocks to put together the grave site.

For a short while, the pair didn't speak and only gathered up stones, slipping them into their bags. After a bit when their bags were about half-filled, Wallais was the first to break the silence.

"It isn't what I imagined it to be like out here," he admitted.

"What were you expecting?"

"To be honest, I thought it would be all sand and dead plants. The way that the Elders advised against coming out here, you would think that that's how it would look."

"Yeah, I suppose you're right. I'd be lying if I didn't say I thought something similar, though I thought it was more of a gas in the air that just killed you."

"Who's to say that there isn't?" Wallais teased.

Lance grabbed at his throat, sticking out his tongue as he feigned death from the invisible gas. He rose to his feet again, both men chuckling to themselves. Lance stopped as a sudden feeling of guilt took him over. His father wasn't dead for more than a day and he was laughing again. He sighed and fought back the stinging feeling of tears threatening to make their presence known.

"Dude, you can let yourself smile," Wallais said.

Lance shrugged. "It just doesn't feel right to me. I feel wrong laughing and joking after everything that's happened. After what I did to that guy last night. Wallais, I butchered a man in cold blood. I was covered head to toe in another man's blood."

Wallais stepped in front of Lance, stopping him in his tracks. He had a serious look on his face and his arms crossed. As memory served for Lance, every time that Wallais had that face on, he meant business and there was no stopping him.

"I think now more than anything is the right time to laugh. I don't know about you, but whenever I laugh if I'm feeling bad I tend to start feeling better. Don't think of it as something to feel bad about, but something to help you feel *better*, especially in a dark time like this. Anyone in your shoes would have done the same thing. What you saw, what you went through in that cabin, it amazes me that you're up and walking around right now."

Lance met his friend's eyeline and let his words soak in. Looking back on all the hard times they went through from dealing with Jasper to comments from both Outsiders and Founders, deaths in both of their families, and more. The one thing they had in common, besides being together for it all, was that they found something to laugh about to help pick up the spirits of the other person. He smiled at his friend, no not friend, his brother.

"I don't know where I would be without you," Lance exasperated with a tearful smile.

"Probably moping around picking up rocks alone. Now you can be moping and picking up rocks with me," he grinned.

"Let's go," Lance chuckled, playfully punching Wallais in the arm, who then feigned that he was severely injured, insighting another laugh from both of them. As the next couple of hours passed by, they chatted together as always, making jokes at each other's expense so that they could get another laugh from one another. Once their bags were heavily weighed down with rocks, they trudged back to the shed to set up for the funerals.

When they returned, the solemn feeling took them over again. Shushannah was seated against the outside wall of the shed with a silent and unmoving face with Adelade in her lap, resting her head on Shushannah's shoulder. Seamus and Ogden were pacing back and forth while Beatrice was inside of the shed cataloging their supplies. Jasper was nowhere in sight, but Lance couldn't have cared less. He was still irritated with him for leaving all the work up to him and Wallais.

Both Lance and Wallais dropped the rocks with a heavy thud on the ground. Jasper came out from around the back of the shed, holding the fabric-wrapped head of his father. Lance would have said something, but Adelade's face was turned in the opposite direction. Jasper trudged over to Wallais and Lance and gently set down his father's head with a sniffle.

The trio began to work in silence, stacking the rocks to create two small shrines to honor their loved ones. Jasper had placed the head of his father in the center before stacking the last of the rocks, finalizing the graves while Lance had placed a pile of folded clothes belonging to his father inside of the shrine he built.

In order to mark them, Lance grabbed four sticks and bound them together with fabric from some rags to make crosses. He placed one on top of the pile for his father while Jasper placed the other on Maxwell's grave. As Lance plunged the sticks into the rocks he couldn't help but feel his anger rise again. He wanted nothing more than to go back to the Community and kill the remaining Tested. He didn't understand how a person could do that to someone else. It was an atrocity.

Silent, heavily wracking sobs took over his body, mourning the realization that he would never see his father again. He was joined by his mother, Adelade, and soon the entire group. They stood in silence, looking at the graves.

Every single person standing around the graves were crying. Lance looked at his mother, tears streaming down her face. He wanted to hug her, but he remembered the one and only time he tried to comfort her and how it went. A part of him almost reached out anyways, but to his surprise, she reached out to him instead. She pulled him into a tight embrace along with Adelade, and they stayed that way, holding each other and crying. Eventually, he pulled away, wiping away tears and mucus from his face. He continued to sniffle, as did those around him. With one final sniff, he grounded himself and turned away from the funeral and walked back to the shed.

A minute later everyone else followed him in, all sharing the same reddened and puffy eyes. Shushannah came in the back holding Adelade as if she were an over-sized toddler.

"Okay," she sighed while adjusting Adelade, "We need to come up with a plan. We need to all agree on how to move forward from here."

"I say we go find Rosalie like we said before," Lance suggested.

"Who's that?" Ogden asked.

"When Lance and I were first out here we were followed by a pair of Tested. She saved us and made sure we got back to the Community in one piece," Shushannah explained.

"How do we find her?" Ogden continued.

Lance pulled a map from his pocket and put it down on the table. "With this. She marked on our map where she and her people are located."

"How do we know we can trust her? How do you know she isn't one of *them*?" Seamus interjected.

Shushannah turned her head towards him. "If you were there with us you would know. I can vouch for her. If there was even a sliver of doubt I wouldn't agree to bring you all there."

Seamus was silent, his concerns answered.

"So that's it then? Are we all in agreement to see if Rosalie will take us in?"

A quiet murmur settled around them, but nobody outwardly denied to seek her out.

"Alright then. We set out tomorrow. I think we should get our bearings and head out first thing tomorrow morning."

Lance suddenly felt the need to get away from everyone. He needed to go clear his head the way that he knew best. "I'll be back," he muttered, slipping away and heading off towards the woods. He knew of the dangers and kept his bow and arrows with him. He wouldn't go far and he wouldn't be long he promised himself. He just needed to go somewhere quiet for a bit to process the events from last night and now today.

He picked a sturdy oak tree and clambered up onto one of the higher branches with a better view of his surroundings. He rested his back against the rough bark and felt his body's natural balance keep him in place on the branch. He sighed, watching steam rise from his mouth and then dissolve away into the cold air. His thoughts wandered away from him as he focused on the cold sting of the wind passing over him with no buffer. He closed his eyes and found his thoughts again. Memories bubbled to the surface of time spent with his father as a child when his mother would go hunting. They were early memories, so early that Adelade wasn't around and it was just him and his father.

The two of them had just finished breakfast together and went down to the grow room. At the time, the plants in the grow room were massive, and to Lance with his short stature at the time, it looked like a jungle. He would weave through the foliage, a deep, healthy green that was only days from bearing fruit. He would pretend he was an explorer looking for treasure, trying to find his way through a labyrinth that seemed to never end. He would spend hours down there while his father worked, but on this day in particular, his father joined him to find this treasure hunt. Together they crawled along the dirt-covered floor, pretending to cross dangerous rivers and fight off tigers until they finally found the treasure they were looking for.

The treasure, in which his father provided, were two ruby red apples from some of the orchards they were able to grow in the greenhouse which they both happily dined on. Lance remembered thinking about how much fun it was to go on the adventure with his father and wished that they could do it in real life.

He wiped away a tear, wishing he could go back to that day and live in the memory forever.

"Hey," a voice below called up to him, "Can we talk for a moment?"

He looked down to see his mother looking up at him.

"Sure," he answered. He let his body slip from the tree and landed gracefully on his feet. He adjusted his bow before leaning against the oak tree in a standing position.

His mother sighed and looked at the ground, looking through her mind for the right words to say. Finally, she stopped and looked Lance in the eyes. "I'm sorry that I wasn't the mother you needed growing up. I was nothing like your father. I know you favored him over me, and you probably still do. I have never blamed you for that. I think that's why I'm so different with Adelade. I feel like I failed you and I don't want to fail her. I made a promise to myself to not be like my father, and I was his exact copy with you."

Lance agreed with his mother, but *only* to an extent.

"Mom, you didn't fail as a parent. I love you just as much as Dad. Sure, Dad and I had the same relationship you have with Adelade, but I feel like lately you and I have gotten closer. I trust you with my life, Mom. You and I were the *first* people of the Community to go past the Edge and into the Wild. We faced the Tested together. You and I got Wallais and his family out of the Alabaster Rampart together. Just because the surface of the relationship looks different doesn't mean it isn't as strong."

"Thank you, Lance, but I want to have a relationship with you more like what you had with your father. You deserve it. You deserve to be treated like a son."

Lance didn't know what to say. He wasn't expecting to have this conversation with his mother at all, but nonetheless he appreciated her making the effort to come over and say the things she did. He wasn't sure if they should hug, so he let her take the lead by simply saying, "Thank you. I'd like that."

She nodded and gave him a smile before she left him.

He buried his face in his hands and slowly dragged them down, pulling on his cheeks, and letting out a groan. There was too much going on today for him to process.

He slumped against the tree and pulled out the crumpled map from his pocket. He looked over the drawings and finally rested his eyes on Rosalie's drawing. He wondered what it was like to live with her people. The more he thought about it, the more he realized that it was going to be much harder to live out here than it was in the Community. There was a lot more to contend with out here besides starvation and greedy, nepotistic leaders. However, that being said, she grew up in a world with these dangers unlike Lance who was learning as he went. He was sure she was fine. She had to be. Right?

He needed to stop thinking in general. It was stressing him out more. He was beginning to realize it was a mistake to come and think. It had done him no good.

He started crossing the field over to the shed when he heard thudding feet rushing up behind him. He turned and ducked, just narrowly dodging a club that was dead-set on connecting with the back of his head. It didn't take him long to realize it was a member of the Tested when he saw the scarred forearm attached to the club.

He drove his right shoulder into the gut of the man, knocking him down and causing the club to spill from his hands. He pinned the man down and began to punch him repeatedly. His fist only managed to connect three times before the man returned a blow with a freed right arm, knocking Lance over. Before he could react, the man had snagged the little club and slammed it down in the center of Lance's forehead, knocking him out cold.

He came to when the sun was beginning to set. He squinted as the beams of orange light pierced his sensitive pupils. His head was pounding and he felt dizzy. He had been put on his knees with his hands bound by rough rope. He blinked repeatedly to clear his blurry vision and shook his head to clear his disorientation.

When he could see again, he realized that everyone was in the same position as him and chained together uncomfortably at the ankles, shoeless, in a single-file line. He had Beatrice on his right and Jasper on his left. Standing in front of them was Bastion with a devilish grin on his face.

"Well, hello everybody," he gushed with more enthusiasm than Lance cared for, "I thought we had lost you all yesterday, but it appears that we didn't after all!"

Bastion began to pace back and forth as he continued to speak. Lance's eyes tracked him with a seething hatred, wanting to get out of his bindings. He wanted to rip the face off of the man responsible for his father's death with his bare hands.

"I'm sad to say that you missed the party last night after we finished rounding up the rest of the people in your little city. I thought the wooden houses were quite adorable, but they were very flammable, which is so impractical when you really think about it. If we hadn't rolled through, something else would have happened anyways. But I digress, I am getting off-topic here. I know this group is responsible for the death of quite a few of my men, *you* especially," he stated pointing at Lance, "You did quite a number on one of them. But I'm feeling generous today. I'll give you all two options: you can either perform the Test and join our ranks, proving your eternal loyalty to myself and our cause, or you can come back to our stronghold where you will perform manual labor in exchange for food, water, and shelter until you die."

He looked up and down the line, both hands up to emphasize his offer. When nobody took him up on it he looked offended.

"Well, that's quite a surprise. Normally there's at least one person that takes me up on that offer, but whatever. I hope you all appreciate what I'm doing here considering you all ran, deserting your people, killing mine, and then proceeding to attack another one of my men moments ago!"

Lance heard a scoff at the end of the line on his right. His head snapped down to his mother, as did everyone else's. She had a smug look on her face and a glint in her eyes that told Lance she was not going to be stepped on by these men.

"What was that?" Bastion questioned moving down the line.

"I think what you're saying is bullshit. You killed my husband, attacked us, burned down our home, and *you* think *we* owe *you* something? Go fuck yourself and fuck your *cause*, whatever the hell that is."

Lance's eyes bulged from his head. Bastion reacted similarly with his mouth agape, just as bewildered as the others. "Excuse me?" Bastion slowly walked over to Shushannah looking back in disbelief at the line of men standing silently and staring straight ahead. He looked over his shoulder at the grave sites and turned back, yet again with a smile on his face.

"It's a scary thing to love something that death can steal away from you, but if he died he was weak and deserved to die. Are your kids here now? I bet the little girl over here is yours. What a little cutie."

"Get away from her you shithead," she growled.

"What's your name?" he barked, no longer in a smiling mood.

"Shushannah."

He snorted. "You have spunk. That won't do. Traeger, get a fire going and when you do, put your knife blade in it. I'm going to need it."

A man missing an arm stepped out of line and scurried off to begin starting a fire. Bastion sat down in front of Shushannah with his legs crossed. They stared each other down while Lance watched the fire in the back grow larger and larger. It was about twenty or so feet away but he could feel the heat radiating from it, which under different circumstances would have been appreciated, but he couldn't focus on the warmth with the threat of his mother being taken from him. He could hardly handle the death of his father, how could he deal with his mother being dead *and* help Adelade through it all? He needed her more than ever. What the *fuck* was she doing?

After a while, the one-armed man came back and whispered something into Bastion's ear, which made him smile. Lance was beginning to learn that when Bastion smiled it was *never* a good thing.

"Since I am in such a forgiving mood today, I'll let you keep your life, but do not mistake my forgiveness for leniency. I can't have you mouthing off anymore. Words can hold a lot of power." He snapped his fingers. "Grab her and bring her over to the fire."

Two Tested broke from the line and unhooked Shushannah from the metal ankle shackles and dragged her over to the massive bonfire. She kicked and struggled, but there was no breaking free for her. Bastion strolled over after casting a smug look over his shoulder at Lance and the others. As he walked, he slipped a knife from his boot and twirled it carelessly in his hands. He stepped up to Shushannah who was now forced onto her knees and casting a dirty look up at Bastion.

Lance could only helplessly look on at the events that unfolded next.

"Since you appear to have the most fire out of everyone, you must e the leader of this little group. I can't have you talking back to me, and I *especially* can't have you inciting a riot among the group. Your name actually gave me an idea on how to hush you up. Open her fucking mouth."

The two men pried open Shushannah's mouth despite her struggling. Bastion stuck his knife into her mouth along with his free hand, pulling her tongue forward. Lance watched in disgust as Bastion sawed through his mother's tongue with her cries of pain echoing through the air. Tears ran down his face from frustration about not being able to do anything. When Bastion finished, he casually threw her tongue into the fire. Dark red blood mixed with saliva dripped from her mouth, down her chin, and onto her shirt. She was breathing heavily with audible groans.

Bastion bent over and smiled inches from Shushannah's face. "That's better," he drolled.

She spat blood back into his face, startling him. He angrily wiped his face. "You bitch," he spat back. He reached down into the fire and pulled out a metal blade that was adorned with an angry red tip. He shoved the metal into Shushannah's mouth, causing her to scream again. Lance could hear cooking flesh as if a raw piece of meat was dropped onto a searing hot pan. He could see steam rising from inside of her mouth as the hot metal closed her wound. When Bastion was done he threw the knife off to the side and punched Shushannah in the face three times, rendering her unconscious. "Take this bitch back to her spot in line. I don't want to fucking look at her anymore."

The two men dragged Shushannah back and replaced the shackles on her legs. Bastion again stood in front of the captured group with a calmer disposition after taking a deep breath.

"I trust that I have made enough of an example for the rest of you to know that I'm serious. I am a very creative person and I can promise, no not promise, *guarantee*, that I can find a suitable punishment for anyone else that feels they can start a rebellion. Of course, where you're all going will break your spirits enough. Tomorrow morning at first light we're heading to your new home." He smiled evilly. "And we'll be sure to have some fun on the way there too."

As the day faded into night, Lance and the others watched helplessly as the Tested went through their things they didn't want and tossed them into the fire where his mother's tongue had long since been turned to ash. He watched their mannerisms, or lack thereof, as he acted as if he were asleep. These men, only men oddly enough, sat around the massive fire, some cooking meat they scrounged from the woods while others just stared into it without moving a muscle. They spoke only when spoken to, and that was only if a question was asked. They obeyed with no question—ultimate loyalty. Bastion was the only person to speak, and when he did, it was the grandeur of a world he wanted in his vision. A world controlled by the Tested.

At one point during the day, he approached the women of the group and explained what their roles *could* have been if they joined, which were essentially birthers or his personal maids. He then explained that children born into their community didn't have to prove their loyalty until they came of age. When they did, they would need to prove their loyalty by both performing a sacrificial killing and carving off of a piece of flesh. As he said it, he said it with sickening pride.

Lance kept to his thoughts while making these observations. What did Bastion have to endure to believe that loyalty was proven by self-mutilation? How bad was this world that this man believed this manner of life and adapted it as the *only* way of life?

Bastion was hard to get a read on. On the surface, he obviously was a power-hungry mongrel. He loved having power and he loved *flexing* that power. He constantly snapped orders, making his men dote on him hand and foot. That being said, there wasn't a whole lot more to see with Bastion. He wanted to be treated like a king, but a child-like king that became irate at a moment's notice.

Just as Bastion said, at sunrise, the line was forced onto their feet and began walking to their destination. The chains around Lance's ankles were already beginning to rub away his flesh. He had started to walk with a limp that had made some of their captors chuckle. He kept his head down and ignored them, chewing the inside of his mouth as anger continued to brew within him. He didn't want to end up being made into an example like his mother.

Lance and the rest of the captives were forced to walk well into the afternoon. By the time they stopped, Lance was ready for a drink. His stomach had been growling heavily, but he was used to the empty feeling. It was the thirst that was bothering him the most, with his tongue sticking to the inside of his mouth like glue. He felt exhausted and his blood was crusting onto his exposed flesh from the chains. They were primitive, but there was no way he was breaking himself or the others out of them without making a lot of noise.

They were finally allowed to stop when Bastion wanted lunch.

After Bastion ate some delectable smelling meat, he allowed some food to be passed down the line. Since their hands were bound, their captors fed them by hand. Lance refused, disgusted by the filthy fingernails of the man offering him the food. He wasn't that hungry yet. He was more hopeful that some water would have been offered as he watched the men sip water from pouches longingly while licking his lips.

Bastion noticed this—much to Lance's dissatisfaction. He waltzed over with his pouch of water. He bent down to Lance's eye level and grinned. "Are you thirsty my friend?" he asked, raising the water. Lance looked Bastion in the eye and then down to the water. "I'll give you a drink," Bastion taunted as he dumped the water into the dirt below. The droplets of water slapped against the soil, puddling faster than it could be absorbed into the ground. Lance watched in horror as the last few drops of water eked out of the spout of the pouch. "Drink," Bastion commanded.

Lance didn't take a sip from the shrinking puddle and instead turned his head away. He didn't want to stoop to that level, plus there was no telling what he could ingest from the soil particles.

"NO," Bastion roared, pulling Lance's hair roughly and putting his face down into the muddied soil, "Drink the fucking water or I'll make sure this is all you have to drink when you get to the Stronghold!"

Lance winced but didn't make a noise. He looked down at the puddle and pursed his lips, sucking up the gritty water. He swallowed it and heaved but managed to keep it down. Vomiting into Bastion's face would *not* be a good thing. He looked away from Bastion's gloating face and tried to ignore the crunchy soil granules now stuck in between his teeth.

"Good," Bastion purred without looking away from Lance, "Get up everyone. Time to keep going."

Everyone got to their feet and continued shuffling along.

"Hey, fuck those guys," Jasper whispered, trying unsuccessfully to pick up Lance's mood.

"Yeah," Lance mumbled back, ending the interaction before it was noticed by the Tested.

They trudged on through the cold for another few hours until the mid-afternoon when Bastion ordered them all again to stop. They were standing in front of what looked like a wall of trees. There was a small entrance just large enough for one person to get through with a well-used dirt path. Lance tried to peer down the path, but it was too far for him to see where the path led to exactly. He couldn't see around that well around them either as the trees were so densely populated they blocked out anything over twenty feet away.

Bastion paced up and down the line with his hands behind his back. Lance was beginning to understand that Bastion *really* enjoyed hearing the sound of his voice. He reminded him of Sampson—if Sampson was a deranged maniac.

"In a few minutes we will be arriving at your new home. When we get there, you will be expected to speak only when spoken to. If you are caught attempting to escape you will be killed on sight. You will receive a work package first thing in the morning and will work until the afternoon where you will be given food and water, at which time you are then expected to work until sunset. Your days will begin at sunrise. You are expected to work every day, and should you not be able to work further due to injury, illness, or the like, you will be killed on the spot, so don't think you can play hookie." He ended his sentence with a wink.

Lance's stomach twisted into knots. He was out of the frying pan and into the fire.

"I will be showing you to your quarters where you will spend your time when not working. You will approach the door to your quarters one at a time while we remove your shackles and bindings." He cocked his head towards the pathway, putting the Tested and the captives into motion. The Tested split their numbers in half and acted as herders for the front and back of the line as they began their journey through the tree tunnel.

As they walked on, Lance tried to use his peripheral vision to see what was around them, but it was no use as the trees still blocked most of his view.

After about ten more minutes they broke free from the trees and entered a clearing that contained a massive factory surrounded by a field of dead sunflowers. He could hear clanking of metal against rock, running machinery, and voices on top of voices reverberating around in the air. Bastion laughed loudly as he stood in front of the line.

With his hands raised triumphantly in the air, he yelled, "Welcome to the Stronghold!"

Lance thought of his father and promised himself that he wouldn't let the Tested break him and that he would avenge his death one way or the other. His eyes lingered on Bastion who looked disappointed as if he expected applause for what he was presenting them with.

I'll kill him. I'll kill every last one of them, he thought to himself. Then the line began to move and he marched forward towards destiny already creating a plan in his mind to break free and put an end to the Tested for good.

END OF BOOK I

ABOUT THE AUTHOR

Doug Anderson is a Rhode Island native, he grew up in Warwick and now lives in Cumberland with his wife and (only slightly psychotic) dog. In 2018, he graduated from Rhode Island College with a Bachelor of the Arts Degree in English Literature. When he isn't reading or writing, he can be found watching horror movies, playing video games, or out taking pictures.

Made in United States
North Haven, CT
04 November 2022

26298813R00104